Book 1

Cozy Mystery Series

Corpse Pose, Indeed

By Jacqueline M. Green

Dedicated to my daughter, that she always keeps her eyes open for a good mystery and knows that dreams do come true.

Thank you to my family and friends, particularly Kelly and Tracy, for encouraging me and reading for me. Thank you to all the writers in my circle for your gentle (but firm) critiques, your encouragement and for laughing at all the right parts.

Chapter 1

The gum-snapping during *savasana* worked on my last nerve. Sitting on my mat at the front, I scanned the class to make sure everyone was lying comfortably during the final minutes of meditation. My students had worked hard. They deserved this peaceful time during the last few minutes of class.

I loved this part of class – sitting quietly, brimming over with gratitude that after so many years I finally owned my own yoga studio, The Yoga Mat. Tonight, I had the bonus feeling of giving back because this class was a fund-raiser for a local nonprofit group that helped women and children. I glanced at the stack of baby blankets and other infant gear in the lobby. My students had gone all out for Safety Blanket.

But that *gum*.

It came from the direction of one of the new students. I didn't want to call her out for it on her first time here, but apparently, the studio needed a larger "no food or gum" sign at the entrance. I couldn't tell if the gum-smacking disturbed Patricia, who lay nearby facing away from me toward the back of the room. Patricia, a regular at the studio, was here to help represent Safety Blanket. Her sister had approached The Yoga Mat to set up the fundraiser, then learned she would be out of town, so Patricia had stepped up.

I gingerly picked up the bell in front of me. Gently ringing it three times invited students out of their meditation. Then I quietly ran through the instructions to stretch and return to a seated position.

"Thank you all for coming to class tonight. I am so grateful for all of the donations to Safety Blanket and all the good energy we are helping to spread," I began. "Let's end our time together with that Sanskrit word 'namaste,' which means-"

"Oh my god, she's not breathing!" A voice interrupted from the back of the room. Students turned to look and several got up and moved toward the form still lying on her mat. They shook their heads at me.

I scrambled to my feet, stepping around yoga mats as I hurried to the back of the room, almost positive that I would find my student breathing after all.

They stood around Patricia, still on her side facing the back, although I could see as I walked nearer that her legs were not gently stacked but looked falling over. Slipping down to my knees, I gently called her name. "Patricia, Patricia?" Carefully placing her head by Patricia's mouth and then her chest, I realized Patricia indeed was not breathing.

"Call 9-1-1!" I barked, then spoke toward the woman on the mat. "Patricia, are you okay? Can I help you?"

When she didn't respond, I started pumping on her chest, glad that I had regular CPR training. I put my ear to her face. Nothing. Despair welled up inside as I started the process again. I'd been teaching yoga for seven years and never had to give CPR to a student before.

From what seemed like far away, I heard someone moving the students out of the classroom. Even farther away, sirens sounded. The clomp of boots let me know paramedics were in the room and I sat back on my heels, then moved away so they could work on her.

My attention turned to the students crowded into the small lobby. "Thank you for your help," I murmured quietly as I moved from person to person, stopping when I reached a sheriff's deputy briskly walking through the front doors.

"Josie, what are you doing here?"

"I heard there was a nonresponsive person at the studio, so I came down. Who is it?"

I leaned in close to her so I could speak softly, placing a hand on her arm. "Thank you. It's Patricia McMillan. Do you know her?"

Josie shrugged. "I could pick her out of a line-up, but I don't know her that well."

Josie looked around the crowded lobby. Some people underestimated the deputy because of how pretty she was, but I knew she didn't miss a detail. "Big class."

"It's the Safety Blanket fund-raiser."

Realization dawned on Josie's face and she nodded, remembering the announcements she had heard in class last week. Josie came to yoga in fits and starts, no matter how often I regaled her with yoga's benefits.

I sucked in my bottom lip and leaned toward her. "Maybe it was a heart attack?"

She shrugged again. "We won't know until we get her to the hospital." She noticed movement in the studio and lifted her face to speak over the students. "Please step aside and allow the medical team to bring the patient out." She started hustling people aside and out the door.

Turning from Josie, I approached a handful of women still clustered together just inside the lobby door. Most of them were also connected to Safety Blanket, including Jennifer, their director, her eyes wide.

"Jennifer, I'm so sorry about Patricia." My arms draped around her in a gentle hug. I stood back to look at her. "I don't know what to say."

Jennifer nodded. "Is she going to be okay?"

I didn't have an answer for her. I knew Patricia hadn't been breathing while I performed CPR and could only hope that the EMTs could bring her back. I looked her in the eyes. "Let's assume everything will be okay until it's not."

She nodded as tears welled up in her eyes, then her gaze went behind my shoulder. The EMTs had the gurney at the wide, arched door.

Silence fell as we watched it bump through the lobby. I scanned Josie's face for signs of a positive turn of events, but her face was closed down and she didn't make eye contact. That wasn't good.

I turned back to Jennifer and we made arrangements for me to deliver the donations to Safety Blanket later in the week. As each woman left, I gave them a quick hug, then I sat down hard on a chair in the lobby. My eyes drifted toward the spot in the studio where Patricia had lain.

Well, *crumb.*

Tracks of dirt showed where the EMTs had walked and rolled the gurney. After a quick glance at the clock showed how precious little time I had before the Restorative class, I jumped up and ran for the closet, jerking out the large broom and a mop, and went to work at hyper speed.

When I was satisfied that the floor was clean enough, I wrung out the mop and threw everything back into the closet. Leaning against the closed door, I blew out a breath just as the front door opened and the first students for the next class stepped inside the lobby.

I was able to gently guide them away from the still-damp area and by the time class had filled up, the area was dry and students readily put down their mats.

Restorative Yoga was one of my most popular classes. Students used many of the studio's props, including the bolsters, and rarely got up off the mats during the meditative class. Nearly an hour later, as students entered *savasana*, the front door swung open and several sheriff's deputies entered the lobby.

I jumped up and hurried across the floor, holding my pointer finger to my lips in the international *shhhhh* signal. Then I made signs to step back outside, which they did reluctantly.

"What's going on?" I asked in a hushed voice.

"Ma'am, we're-" started one deputy loudly.

"Shhh, the door is not soundproof and my students are in *savasana*."

He looked at me blankly. "Ma'am, I have no idea what that means, but we need to get inside the studio tonight, as in, right now."

"Why?"

Josie arrived just then, breaking through the others. She put a hand on my shoulder and looked me in the eye. "Mariah, Patricia died, but the doctors say it looks suspicious."

"Suspicious? What do you mean, suspicious?"

"Patricia was probably murdered."

My mouth fell open. I stared at Josie, who silently nodded back.

"Wh-what happens now?"

Another deputy stepped forward. "What happens is we need access to your studio right now to look for evidence."

I looked at the door as if I could see through it. "We have about a minute left in this class. Can I finish and send everyone home?"

Josie and the other deputy exchanged a look. "Yes, but I'll need to make a note of who is here and who was here during your last class."

I reached for the door, then turned back, giving them the "wait here" sign. Josie ignored it and stepped in behind me. She stood at the doorway, arms folded and back straight as I quietly finished the class, then watched as students put away the bolsters and blocks. As they left, she took down their names and phone numbers before they walked through the door.

"You know I already have a list of who is in the class, Josie. They sign in when they get here. You've done it yourself."

Josie nodded without looking at me. "I know, Mariah, but this lets me see first-hand who was here."

"But they weren't even in that class."

"They are connected to the studio, so I would be remiss if I didn't note their names."

"Remiss?" I heavy-sighed at her and bit back another response, opting instead, "Is there anything I can do?"

"Besides quit talking to me while I work?"

I sucked in my lip again and stared at Josie, who finally smirked even as she took the next woman's phone number. "Look, Mariah, why don't you draw a diagram of where everyone was during Patricia's class, whose mats were closest to her, that kind of thing? Also," she checked her watch. "You'll need to cancel the 7 a.m. class while we figure out what we have here."

Josie got one more stink eye from me, then I turned into my small office, tucked off a corner of the lobby. Flipping on the laptop, I typed "Morning Flow is cancelled today." As I began to add "Sorry for the inconvenience," I paused. Surely a death in my studio ranked higher than "inconvenient." Instead, I added "Check the website for updates" and hit "print" While it printed, I updated the website and social media pages, hoping most students would see the information so they didn't show up for class. Then snagging the paper from the printer, I slipped around Josie and taped it to the inside of the front glass door.

I bit back a frown as I thought about the cancelled class. Morning Flow was popular with several regulars, making it was one of my more consistent and profitable classes. As a small-business owner, I hated to cancel a moneymaker. As a, well, *person,* I knew it was the right thing to do.

Pulling another sheet of copy paper from the office printer, I sketched rectangles where I remembered everyone was in class, murmuring to myself. "Patricia was over here, Stormy and her gum were over here." I was sure where Stormy McMaster was, and I was nearly sure she was the one with the gum.

A man's voice intruded from the doorway. "I thought yoga was supposed to be healthy."

Chapter 2

A man's voice intruded on my work from the doorway and because it was a smart-aleck thing to say, I held up my pointer finger in the international sign for "wait a minute, jerk." Actually, the "jerk" part might not be internationally known, but I added it in my head, then filled in the name on the last mat and looked up.

A man – mid-forties, with blond hair that curled slightly a little too much over his collar to be strictly regulation – leaned against the doorjamb. He held a small notebook in one hand, a sheriff's badge in the other.

I headed up to the high road and ignored his comment. "Can I help you, deputy?"

He nodded. "Detective Samuelson, ma'am. And you are?"

"Mariah Stevens. I own this studio and you must be the 'new guy'."

"Ouch?" A smile touched his lips.

"Sheriff Cynthia Stevens is my sister. I'm pretty sure you already know that. I'm quite familiar with the staff at the Jasper County Sheriff's Department."

Samuelson inclined his head to acknowledge my statement, then opened his notebook. "Okay if I ask a few questions?"

I nodded and sat back in my chair, crossing my arms over my chest. Cindy would probably call this a defensive position, but I needed the comfort of my own hug. The detective leaned against the door jamb, since I had no other seats in the room. Most of the business I conducted in the office was financial, such as when students paid for classes. A handful of foldable chairs stood in the corner for those occasions I had an activity that warranted them, but mostly my students sat on their mats when they were here.

The detective's eyes flickered to the chairs, then away, as he sighed and got down to business.

"Where were you when the victim was found?"

Victim. How sad to think of Patricia that way. "I taught the class when Patricia, um, I don't know what happened to her."

"She died."

"Of course." My hug got a little tighter as I nodded. "How?"

He looked at me with a strange expression, his blue eyes glinting in the lamplight. "I kind of hoped you could shed some light on that." He tapped his notebook. "Why don't you tell me what happened?"

I told him what I knew, which frankly was precious little. I had led the 14 students through an ordinary all-levels *vinyasa* class, then moved into *savasana* for the last few minutes. *Savasana*, as I explained to the detective, was that five or six minutes of meditation time at the end of class when students relax on their mats. For many of my yoga students, it's their favorite time of the class.

"Isn't that called corpse pose?" the detective asked more to himself than to me, grimacing. "Ironic."

I paused and eyeballed him, my mouth pursed like a cranky librarian, but I could not ignore a flip comment for the second time.

The detective froze when he saw me watching him, then had the grace to blush. "I apologize," he said. "Gallows humor, I guess, but I realize … I … um."

Satisfied, I brushed away his apology with my hand. I just wanted to move on and finish this interview.

I hadn't noticed anything different about Patricia tonight. She had been coming to class for about four months now. Her sister, Melinda, had been a regular since I opened the studio not quite nine months ago and had brought her as a guest.

"Someone needs to tell Melinda." I knew Josie had a lot on her plate and I didn't want the Sheriff's Department to forget to let her know. To be honest, I just hoped I wasn't the one expected to take care of that particular task.

To my great relief, the detective reached at a hand as if to stop me from leaping from my chair to call Patricia's sister. "We've got that covered, Ms. Stevens. Thank you. You were saying?"

Patricia had mentioned recently that she'd had stomach pains and some nausea. I'd suggested modifications to certain poses in class and encouraged her to see her doctor if it kept up.

"Did she ever see her doctor?" The detective stopped writing to look at me.

I lifted my hands to my shoulders in a silent "beats me." Then I explained how being a yoga teacher works in the real world.

"A lot of people frequently ask me health questions because I work so much with the body and they perceive me as being healthy. But they don't always take what I say to heart, which is okay because I'm not a doctor. Many are just seeking an opinion that matches what they already think."

"Are you not really healthy? You seem healthy." Those blue eyes looked at me inquisitively.

"That's what you got out of my explanation? Seriously?" I ran my hands through my hair as if I could wash away this night and these questions. To his credit, the detective didn't add "you don't look like a yoga teacher," which I've heard a lot. He waited with relaxed shoulders and raised eyebrows. Finally I looked at him, my patience leaking by the second. "I have my moments. Mostly I seek balance. Can we finish up, please?"

He gestured for me to go on, so I mentioned that Patricia had seemed paler than usual tonight, but I didn't notice anything alarming. Until the part where she stopped breathing.

That was alarming.

"You didn't think it was odd that she didn't get up at the end of class?"

I shook my head. "Sometimes people fall asleep during *savasana*. Usually they wake up when everyone starts moving around. If they don't, I go over and gently wake them. Or, like tonight, someone else notices and wakes them, tries to anyway."

He stopped writing and looked at me, a smile playing at his face. "Isn't that kind of bad form, to fall asleep during—"

"*Savasana?*" I shrugged. "I don't take it personally. It just means they're tired – and aren't we all sometimes?"

I knew I sounded like the stereotypical yoga teacher, all love and tolerance. Dammit, I just couldn't help it sometimes. I'll admit there were times I wanted to curse a blue streak in front of my students just to see how they'd react.

He closed his notebook and tucked it into his jacket pocket, advising me that he would likely have more questions later once the investigation was further along.

After the sheriff's staff cleared out, I quickly locked the front locks and fled out the back way to my car, parked just beyond the back steps. My yoga studio – all 600 square feet of it – normally was my refuge, a sanctuary from the world. How would it change now that a woman had died there? My head leaned against the steering wheel as tears streamed silently down my face as I sobbed both for Patricia and for the innocence lost in my studio tonight.

My cell phone buzzed. I swiped right and held the phone to my ear. "Cindy?" I sniffed.

"I just heard. I'm gathering information now. I'm so sorry this happened. Are you okay?"

I nodded.

"Did you nod at the phone or shake your head?"

"I nodded. I'm okay, just sad and confused." The truth of my statement surprised even me.

"Lift your head off the steering wheel."

My head flew up in surprise. How did she always know these things?

Tap-tap-tap! I jumped as Cindy's face appeared in the passenger-side window. As I unlocked the doors, she slid into the car and turned her body to face mine.

"I can only stay a minute. We don't get many deaths like this one around here."

She spoke softly, as if someone else was listening, then opened her arms and I leaned into them. "Thank you for covering my class tonight," she said, a smile in her voice.

I groaned. "Next time, get Tabitha to do it." I had almost forgotten that I had been substituting for Cindy, who had helped set up the fund-raiser. In addition to being the county sheriff, she was a certified yoga instructor who taught two classes a week at The Yoga Mat. In fact, she was the one who got me interested in yoga when I was in college. Yoga helped her stay focused while on patrol in San Francisco, her first job out of school.

She sat up and released me, turning my chin so she could look me in the eyes. "Go home. Have a warm bath. Go to bed. There's nothing to be done for Patricia now."

I nodded at her. She bent toward me, kissed my cheek, then pushed open the door and stepped back into the night.

I sat there for a moment, staring at nothing. My phone buzzed again. *Go home.*

Oh, for Pete's sake. When your sister is the sheriff, you truly have no privacy.

Arriving home, I knew what had to be done, despite what Cindy had said. Desperate times, desperate measures and all that.

Dropping my bag and shoes in the front hallway, I headed for the bottom shelf of the pantry. Mere moments later, a crumpled bag of reduced-fat potato chips in one hand and a diet soda in the other, my head dropped against the back cushions as I flopped into the couch. Thank goodness for mind-numbing television and channel-surfing.

If only my yoga students could see me now. I crammed another salty chip into my almost full mouth, barely noticing the crunch. Washing it down with a swig of the diet soda, I relished every moment as much as I could after this evening.

My cell buzzed again, jolting me upright until I saw who it was. I clicked on the speaker button and sat back to wait.

"OMG, Mariah, are you OK? I heard about Patricia. What happened? Did Josie come? Was it the Wild Thing pose? I knew that one would kill somebody one day, but actually I thought it would be me. Mariah? Are you there?"

I smiled, listening to my best friend's rant, knowing that CeCe Montgomery was trying to take my mind off the situation in her own caffeinated and wacky way.

"I'm fine. I'm not sure what happened, and, no, it was not the Wild Thing. You only *think* it will kill you, but it won't. It hasn't yet."

"You will never convince me of that."

"Thanks for calling, Cee. I'm going to bed. See you tomorrow?"

"I'll be there. Sleep well."

Though I had said I was going to bed, I tossed and turned, my mind racing with the possible effects Patricia's death could have on my new studio. Jasper wasn't a very big town to begin with and I'd felt lucky to draw in enough students in the first eight months to almost show a profit. Could a student's passing be the death knell for my fledgling studio?

Chapter 3

The next morning, law enforcement officers were in and out, largely ignoring me or simply nodding. I finally stepped from my office and stopped a burly-looking deputy as he entered the front double doors for the second or third time.

"Excuse me, Deputy Alvarez, I'm surprised that the Sheriff's Department is still here. Have there been complications?"

His face was impassive. "You'll need to talk your sister or the detective in charge about that, ma'am."

Well, thank you very much. He turned away and I cringed as he started across the studio floor in his work shoes.

"Deputy Alvarez, can you please remove your shoes before you enter the studio?"

He turned and scowled. "Ma'am, I know your sister is the sheriff, but this is official business."

"I understand, Deputy. However, my students spend a great deal of time on that floor and it needs to be kept as clean as possible. I already had paramedics and sheriff's officers all over it last night."

He shook his head. "So it's already dirty. Ma-"

"Please." I waited, trying to keep my breathing even. Finally, the deputy sighed, sat down on a straight-backed chair in the lobby and unlaced his shoes.

"Thank you. I'd appreciate it if you'd let the others know." I gave a chin-nod toward the other deputies in the room, grateful not only that he took off his shoes but that it didn't become a big power struggle.

Perhaps I'm supposed to be zen and all that, but I hate to back down from a fight. Satisfied that the studio floor wouldn't be trashed while law enforcement did its thing, I slipped my shoes back on and walked to CeCe's Coffee down Main Street.

CeCe's eyes widened when she saw me and she quickly wiped her hands on her apron, then pulled me in a big hug. She pulled back and looked in my eyes. "You okay?"

My body couldn't decide which way to go – nod yes, no, maybe. My hands flailed instead. Smiling gently, CeCe led me to a small table in the back next to the barista's station.

I slumped into the seat, waving to a few people across the tables. Just as a couple stood and began to weave through the tables toward me, CeCe easily stepped in front of them, positioning herself between them and me as she set a mocha and croissant on the table.

"I'll be back," she mouthed to me, then she whipped around and hurried the couple back in the direction from which they had come. CeCe didn't let them stop until the bell over the front door dinged behind them. CeCe stayed at the door and waved until they headed down the sidewalk, then made her way back to me.

"Thank you." I sipped my mocha, noticing she had added a touch of coconut this morning. The croissant had chocolate inside. "I feel spoiled."

CeCe sat down across from me. "I knew you would need chocolate today. Have they told you anything?"

I shrugged as I chewed.

She leaned toward me, lowering her voice. "What I've heard so far is that she was shot with a silencer during your class."

I nearly spit out the croissant, so I stopped to swig down some mocha as CeCe held up her hand.

"No wait, there's more." She ticked them off on her fingers. "It was a mob hit. Patricia was in the Witness Protection Program living here incognito for the past fifteen years and someone finally recognized her." Another finger. "She took poison so she wouldn't have to give up any secrets." Another finger. "She had been hacking into Amazon and they found out." She paused, pressing back her pinky finger as she thought. "No, I guess that's all. Are any of those close to the truth?"

I shrugged again. "They could be, for all I know. Except the one about her being shot with a silencer. She wasn't shot. There was nothing that looked like she was about to die."

Just then my phone buzzed. I checked the messages and frowned, looking up at CeCe. "The new Sheriff's detective wants to talk to me. I'm to meet him back at the studio."

I turned off the phone and set it down, then picked up my mug of mocha.

CeCe smiled. "Is that your way of 'sticking it to the man'?"

A silent toast with the mug, then I picked up my croissant, oozing with chocolate. "I'm fairly sure he can't arrest me for eating breakfast."

"Tell me that's not your breakfast."

"It's not my breakfast?"

CeCe made a face and shook her head. "It's a snack, you yoga goof-off. *Snack*. Breakfast involves fruit, grains and possibly juice. Maybe yogurt in a pinch."

"Ms. Stevens, there's a call for you." CeCe's head barista, Paul, handed me the coffee shop's cordless phone and I put it to my ear.

"Ms. Stevens? It's Detective Samuelson. I'm at your studio. Can you meet me here to discuss last night's incident?"

"Of course, Detect-" I shut off the phone before I finished the word and handed it to CeCe, then shoved a last unwieldly bite of croissant into my mouth.

"You gotta go?"

I nodded as I chewed, regretting not breaking the bite into two pieces. When I was finally able, I washed it down with the last of the mocha. I handed the empty cup back to CeCe. "You, my friend, are a lifesaver, a beacon for chocolate lovers everywhere."

CeCe smiled and hitched a thumb over her shoulder toward the door. "I think 'the man' is waiting for you."

I paused, playing with the napkin in my hands. "Say, Ceese?"

CeCe sat back down when she saw my serious expression.

"Who could possibly have wanted to kill Patricia?"

CeCe shrugged. "The Sheriff's Department will find that out."

"I'm worried. I feel like there's more to it, just because, you know, there's a detective waiting for me. Why would he come back to interview me?"

CeCe tapped her fingertips against her lips in thought. Finally, her eyes met mine. "Let's wait and see what he says. There's not much we can do until we know."

"Okay, but The Yoga Mat is not going down without a fight."

CeCe reached over to take my hands in hers. "Agreed."

I squeezed her hands in response, then pressing my hands into the table, I stood up heavily, already regretting the abundance of chocolate just consumed. After a quick hug to CeCe and a wave to Paul, I walked slowly back to my studio. I couldn't shake the feeling that Patricia's death was just the tip of the proverbial iceberg.

Chapter 4

Detective Samuelson sat in my studio lobby, looking crisp and freshly pressed.

"Good morning, Detective."

"I wasn't sure you got my message, Ms. Stevens. Seems like the phone cut out on us."

It wasn't a question, so I didn't feel the need to address it. I would keep my pathetic passive-aggressive ways to myself.

Motioning him into my office, I took a seat behind the desk, just as I had last night. It wasn't so much that I wanted the sense of power but that my office is small. At least, that's what I told myself.

"What can I do for you, detective?"

"First of all, please call me Neil."

"First-name basis? Does that mean I'm not a suspect?"

He grinned. "Everyone's a suspect. It means this is a small town and I like to maintain good relations with folks when I can. May I call you Mariah?"

I tilted my head and studied him curiously. Cindy spoke highly of her new hire, thrilled she had lured him here from the Bay Area. I could probably cut him some slack.

"You may, but only because this is a small town and my sister the sheriff seems to think you're okay. We'll see how it goes."

Neil dipped his head in acknowledgment. He didn't wait for me to offer but went ahead and pulled out one of the folded metal chairs, opening it up and settling onto it. He wiggled his hips a little apparently to get comfortable – not that I was noticing his hip wiggle, of course. He crossed one leg over the other knee, then cleared his throat.

He looked at me across the desk as if weighing what to say. At last he spoke.

"How well did you know the victim?"

"We discussed that last night. I only knew her a little through the studio."

He shrugged and looked at me pointedly. "I thought you might have remembered something last night that would be useful."

I stared at him as the silence grew.

"Oh, right." I knocked my forehead with the palm of my hand. "You mean how I remembered that I killed Patricia in my own studio and then used CPR to try to revive her until the paramedics arrived? Did I forget to mention that last night, detective? *I did, didn't I?*"

He pursed his lips and stared at the ground, then at me, his face solemn. "I'm fairly certain you're being sarcastic right now."

"Ya think?"

He closed his notebook. "Look, Mariah, I know this is hard. Do you think it's easy for me to ask these questions? A woman died. In *your* studio. Do you think this is a joke?"

I blinked first as my cheeks blushed. We sat in silence for a moment. If I could have crawled under my desk without him noticing, I probably would have.

"I'm sorry. You're right. I don't know why I was so flip."

He nodded at me, then reopened his notebook and looked at me expectantly, his blue eyes looking less friendly, not to mention less sparkly. "We're fairly certain that Mrs. McMillan did not die of natural causes."

"How certain is 'fairly certain'?"

"Pretty sure. We sent her body to San Francisco overnight. One of the medical examiners there is a buddy of mine and did an autopsy first thing this morning. Patricia's organs and systems were that of a mostly healthy woman."

I took a deep breath and tried to relax my quickly-tensing shoulders. "So that means she actually *was* murdered."

"It certainly looks that way.

My shoulders slumped and I covered my mouth with my hand. Then I quickly stood up and stepped silently across the floor to the studio doorway, staring at the spot where Patricia's mat had lain. She wasn't one of those students who always had to be in a certain spot. She was happy to mix it up and move around. I liked that about her.

How could something as violent as a murder occur in my peaceful, happiness-seeking yoga studio? That went against everything I – and my yoga practice – stood for.

The detective let that sink in for a few moments, no doubt watching my reaction.

He cleared his throat. "So, Ms. Stevens? How well did you know Mrs. McMillan?"

I thought for another moment standing at the studio doorway, then walked back and returned to my chair behind my desk, rolling the wheels a little.

"When Patricia first started coming here, she seemed lost, like she had no purpose. Her cheeks were usually flushed, so I figured she either drank a bit or perhaps had rosacea or a heart condition. Then after she had been coming to class regularly for a couple of months, she seemed stronger, like she was feeling better about herself. Yoga will do that to a person sometimes."

The detective kept his eyes on me as he wrote without looking at his notebook.

"Did you ever work for newspapers, Detective?"

He shook his head. "Nope, been in law enforcement most of my adult life. Why?"

"A lot of reporters use that trick of writing without looking at the paper."

He glanced at his notes as he spoke. "It's a handy skill. I can also curl my tongue, which is less useful. Anything else you can remember?"

This time, I nodded. "As I mentioned last night, in the past three weeks or so, she started saying she'd been having stomach pains. I suggested modifications to the poses during class, but she kept having pains. Then this week, she didn't have much energy, and she seemed sad."

He paused to look at his notes. "Anything else?"

"She stayed to talk after class one day." I sat back and looked toward the ceiling, trying to picture the conversation. "I think she just wanted to bounce an idea off of someone."

"What idea was that?"

"She was thinking of divorcing her husband."

The detective's eyebrows shot up. "Hmmm," he muttered. "He conveniently left *that* little tidbit out of our interview." His eyes lifted back to mine. "What did she say about that? How serious was she?"

I shrugged. "Serious enough to talk to me about it but also wondering if it was the right thing to do." I hesitated. Was Patricia's story mine to tell the detective? I felt the need to tread lightly.

He noticed my hesitation and settled back into the metal chair, seemingly content to wait. After a few more moments, he spoke. "Mariah, you can't hurt Mrs. McMillan now. She's beyond that."

"I know, I *know*. I just don't want her to look bad. She can't defend herself."

Neil shrugged. "There's no judgment here, Mariah. People are imperfect. You see that in your job as much as I do in mine."

I thought about that. He probably saw quite a bit more imperfect humanness than I did. Imperfection in yoga just meant a different experience, perhaps a different stretch or feeling; it didn't mean jail time.

"She – Patricia – had already been divorced four times and she didn't know if she should do it again. She felt –" again I paused, searching for the right words, letting my fingers bounce lightly on the desk in front of me – "She felt there was something wrong with her for having been married so many times."

I distinctly remembered what she had said to me, tears in her eyes: "What's wrong with me, Mariah? Why can't I be happy with the men I marry? Why can't I stay married?"

The detective nodded, but it didn't seem as if he was judging, more like acknowledging the pain. "What did you tell her?"

"What difference does it make?" I crossed my arms again.

"It might tell us about her state of mind."

I made a face and, no, I'm not proud of that. Then I sat up a little straighter, preparing to be judged for my response.

"I encouraged her to practice *ahimsa* toward herself." His eyebrows raised again. What was it with those eyebrows? "*Ahimsa* is one of the five yamas, um, guidelines, of yoga."

I went on with a quick summary of the practice of *ahimsa*, or non-violence. Essentially, *ahimsa* promotes the practice of compassion and love toward ourselves, each other and the Earth, including by showing forgiveness toward others as well as ourselves.

"Often, we are the most harmful toward ourselves because we place expectations on ourselves and then we beat ourselves up when we don't achieve them." I finished and looked at the detective. Knowing how cynical law enforcement types can be, I was surprised to see compassion on his face.

He pursed his lips thoughtfully. "And yoga helps with that."

I smiled, catching his eyes with mine. "That's not a question. Yes, ideally it does. We learn to be kind to ourselves, to meet ourselves right where we are when we're doing asanas – the physical poses – on the mat." Just telling the detective about *ahimsa* helped me feel better, stronger even.

Bring it on, detective. I can handle anything now.

His lifted his eyes to meet mine. "Did you find Patricia's water bottle from last night?"

"No," I said slowly. "Now that you mention it, I don't remember seeing it last night."

I frowned at the sudden change in subject, glancing around the office to see if someone had set the water bottle inside. The detective's eyes followed me as I walked back into the studio and looked at the spot where she had lain, even though I knew it wasn't there, then back to the cubbies in the front lobby, where students left their shoes and purses.

"That's weird. I'm sure she had it with her when she came to class yesterday. I seem to remember her filling it from our water dispenser." I slowly walked back into the office and sat down. "My remembrance of the days could be running together, but it definitely wasn't there when I cleaned last night."

"You cleaned the studio last night?" He sighed heavily, then re-opened his notebook and started writing again. "Before or after the sheriff's team came back?"

"Before, and, of course, I cleaned. EMTs had been walking in and out on the floor in their street shoes. It was a quick sweep and mop, but I had to. I had a class coming in."

He stopped and looked at me again. "I'm sure the team noticed that this morning. I hope you didn't sweep or mop away any *evidence*." He looked at me pointedly.

I blew out a breath and stood up, plunking both hands on my desk. "You can't really think I killed Patricia."

He shrugged, and anger rose inside me. So much for *ahimsa*.

"Why would I kill a paying client? She paid six months in advance."

"Maybe you needed room for another mat?"

"It's a small town, detective. If I started killing clients, I would have to close my studio within a couple of months. How smart would that be?" He didn't reply, so I answered for him. "Not smart at all, *detective*." I emphasized that word this time because at this moment he did not seem like much of one and I wanted to oh-so-subtly let him know.

He just watched me. I could tell he didn't miss much. "The water bottle?"

I pointed to the small water dispenser in the corner of the lobby. "She always had her water bottle with her. It was very distinctive." I started to describe Patricia's bottle, a tall thinner-than-usual tube covered in pink and green Hawaiian flowers, but the detective just frowned at the water dispenser.

"Has anyone else used that water fountain in the past 24 hours?"

I shrugged. "Of course." I picked up my water bottle from the desk and held it up. "I filled mine just a little while ago."

"Did you drink from it yet?"

"What's going on, Detective?" I clutched my water bottle to my chest with both hands. I wasn't afraid of him taking it, but I suddenly felt anxious.

The detective hesitated. "We suspect Patricia was poisoned."

I gasped as if someone had kicked me in the stomach. "How can that be? Who would do something like that?"

"People who kill others do many things I don't understand. Poison makes it particularly problematic to find out who did it."

"Have you talked with her husband? Never mind that question. Of course, you've talked with him. She died over twelve hours ago."

Neil smiled and nodded, then cocked his head to look at me. "You know an awful lot about murder investigations, if you don't mind me saying so."

I shrugged. "My sister is the sheriff."

"So? My sister sells insurance, and I really couldn't tell you anything about it." He smiled a self-deprecating smile, then looked expectantly at me, waiting for me to be more forthcoming. He crossed one well-pressed leg over the other and settled in his chair. Apparently, he really was waiting for an answer.

I met his gaze with one of my own, my hands clasped around the water bottle.

I blinked first, but only so I could get him out of my studio. Not because his blue eyes were gazing into mine.

"I used to be a reporter with a couple of major newspapers. I covered cops and government, so I have an idea how it all works."

He nodded as if I had satisfied his curiosity, but I knew better. This guy was no slouch or Cindy wouldn't have hired him. He did his homework before showing up in my office. "You already knew that." It wasn't a question.

He closed his notebook and tucked it into his pocket and stood up, patting his trousers as if looking for something. "Let me know if that water bottle turns up."

He turned to leave, then paused at the door of my tiny office and looked back at me. He looked at me skeptically. "Mariah, you understand this is a sensitive case, right? Mrs. McMillan died in your studio during your class. You, being the sibling of the sheriff, will be held to the highest standard during the investigation to ensure that no bias is shown. I hate to say this and please don't take it the wrong way, but I will need you to come to the post sometime today to give us fingerprints."

My mouth fell open.

"Any time at your convenience," he rushed to add, then quickly stepped out the door.

The police finally cleared out about noon, taking my water dispenser and water bottle as well as their yellow tape with them. As Deputy Alvarez had paused to sit down and put on his shoes, I hurried to the office door.

"Deputy Alvarez, thank you for your help this morning." I gestured into the studio. "Do you know if I can reopen for business?"

He looked up, one shoe in his hand. My smile greeted his scowl. Then he nodded, the scowl falling off his face as if he had thought better of it.

"Yes, ma'am. We're through in here. We might have more questions, but we've taken all of the physical evidence we can find."

"Thank you." I whispered it softly, feeling a sense of relief that this part of the nightmare was over.

I locked the door behind him and kept the "CLOSED" sign up, then turned from the lobby to stand in the doorway of the studio. The purple bolsters still stood in the corner next to shelves holding green knit blankets and teal-colored blocks. Extra mats stood in a cut-off barrel for students who needed them.

The room looked the same as always but felt off. I shouldn't be surprised. After all, someone had died here.

I pulled my yoga mat out of its cubby. It still smelled like the chemicals the police had used to wipe it down for evidence. I wiped it off with my own familiar lavender cleanser, then placed it in about the spot where Patricia had died. Crossing my legs into a half-lotus, I gently closed my eyes and let my energy slip around me, feeling out the edges of my consciousness.

After several minutes in this meditative state, I felt the hairs on the back of my neck stand on edge and a chill ran down my back.

"Dear Patricia," I whispered into the void. "I don't know why this happened to you or who did it, but I promise you I will find out."

Chapter 5

Cindy and Josie beat me to the diner down the street just after lunchtime. The smell of bacon hit my nose and the bell on the front door jingled when I entered. I didn't dislike the smell, though quitting bacon was my biggest challenge in going vegetarian several years ago. Still, the diner felt homey and the cook was always willing to adjust a meal for me to make it vegetarian.

My sister and Josie had already snagged a booth in the nearly full diner. I slid in next to Cindy and looked across the table at Josie. I knew she had had a late night, with Patricia's death and all, but she still managed to look beautiful, her straight dark hair pulled back in a chignon and makeup artfully done. I peered closer and could tell she had done another amazing job hiding the dark rings under her eyes. It had been a long night for the sheriff's department.

Cindy looked more worn-out but still energetic, as usual. Her wavy blond hair was pulled back in a practical pony tail and reading glasses perched on her nose. Her lipstick, if she had remembered to put it on, had long since rubbed off.

"Long night, ladies?" I asked as I moved the menus aside. We ate there too often to even need them, but the waitress always brought a few.

They both nodded. Josie lifted her coffee mug in a salute. "Whoever discovered coffee should be the patron saint of law enforcement everywhere."

Cindy just smiled, keeping her eyes on the notes in her folder, but I gave it some thought.

"You know, Josie, it's not like explorers went into the jungle and discovered a Mr. Coffee brewing away."

"You know, Mariah, I really don't care." Josie took another sip while I pulled out my cell phone to look it up. I tapped at the screen for a few moments.

"A goat herder!" I exulted, then stopped myself. "Wow, that came out way more excited than I actually feel about it." Josie watched me through tired eyes over her coffee cup. "Apparently, an eleventh century goat herder discovered the coffee plant in Ethiopia. Actually, his goats discovered it."

Josie's eyebrows went up and she saluted silently with her cup. I pressed the home button and cleared the open apps, then set my phone on the table, looking around for the waitress.

Cindy finally looked up at me. "How are you doing, sis? Did they get everything cleared out of the studio?"

I nodded as I waved for the waitress to take our orders. She whipped out her pad and we quickly ordered before she raced off to the next table.

I filled Cindy and Josie in on the morning, including my lengthy conversation with Detective Neil Samuelson.

"Well?" I turned to look at Cindy when I finished.

"Well what?" She took a sip of her coffee as she looked back at me.

"*Well*, what are you going to do about it? He thinks I killed someone."

Cindy thought for a moment, her hand wrapped around her coffee mug. "*Well*, I guess I probably shouldn't be having lunch with a murder suspect. That won't look too good for me at re-election time, which is coming up in a couple of months."

I sat back in my booth and glared at my older sister as a guffaw escaped from Josie. My gaze zinged over to her. "You're actually laughing about this? It's not funny. I don't laugh at you when you do Downward Dog, and I could sometimes, I really could."

"That's fair," Josie shrugged, then she and Cindy burst out laughing.

I sipped the coffee just set down by the waitress. "You're both too punchy to make sense."

Cindy turned serious, leaning toward me so she could speak quietly. "Because we suspect poison, it widens the field of suspects. To poison someone, you don't need to be strong or have good aim."

"But you do have to be able to get close to your victim, right? so wouldn't that narrow rather than widen the field?"

Cindy laid her head comfortably on my shoulder. "You might be right about that, sis. I just have to stay out of it, but truly, don't worry. Neil will dot all the proverbial i's and cross those t's, especially since you're involved and you're my baby sister."

She sat up and turned to look at me, no easy task in booth seats. "It will be uncomfortable for a while, but I know Neil will bulldog this to its rightful conclusion."

I felt a little better. Not a lot, but enough to eat my lunch without feeling like Detective Samuelson was breathing down my neck.

Just then a whir of blue sashayed past our table and scooted in next to Josie.

"About time you showed up," Josie said as CeCe settled into her seat. CeCe just shrugged, then reached for the iced tea Josie had ordered for her knowing that CeCe most likely would be late. Getting away from the Coffee House was often dicey.

CeCe had barely caught her breath when our waitress plopped a full plate in front of her. CeCe didn't miss a beat, just whipped out her napkin with her left hand as she picked up her grilled sandwich with her right, cheese oozing down the sides. She paused to bite off the gooey parts hanging off the side, then looked at me expectantly.

"How are you? Are the cops still in your studio?"

"Sheriff's deputies." Cindy and Josie corrected CeCe automatically. I'm pretty sure CeCe said it on purpose. She gave a slight smile, her eyes flitting back and forth between her sandwich and me.

"I'm fine. For me, it's an inconvenience, of course, but for Patricia and her family, I can't even imagine."

Her eyes finally stopped on my face, sympathy registering. Then she glanced at her watch and took a big bite from her sandwich, now holding it with both hands. Josie and Cindy reached in to steal a chip from CeCe's plate. None of us typically wanted a whole plate of chips, so hers were the agreed-upon trove.

Josie's eyebrows went up as she munched on hers. "What? No chips?" A few stray chip bits fell out of her month.

"Ew, Josie, and no, I climbed into a bag of the ruffled ones last night." I hated to admit it.

All three of my friends – sister included – nodded at me.

"With Diet Pepsi?" CeCe asked. "You've got to eat them with Diet Pepsi. I think it's the combination of the salt from the chips and that sharp fizziness of the Pepsi. The other brands aren't fizzy enough."

I laughed as I nodded, really relaxing for the first time in nearly fifteen hours. I looked around the little table as the other three went off on another topic. They couldn't be more different from each other and from me, for that matter.

Josie, all dark and beautiful, her calm exterior hiding the soul of a cynic. I met Josie through Cindy, of course.

Then my eyes found CeCe, who had befriended me when I first moved to Jasper last year, first as a fellow small business owner and then in true friendship. I needed CeCe's caffeine as much as she needed my yoga. She was the first person to sign up for a six-month pass at my newly opened studio, saying yoga calmed her down after being dunked in caffeine all day. Truly, CeCe was a whirlwind. If yoga could calm *her* down, it could calm anyone.

Josie had grown up in Jasper; her large and extended family still lived here. CeCe was a transplant like Cindy and me, only she came across the country from upstate New York.

"So what are you doing for it?"

"What?" Apparently, I had zoned out as I had basked in the appreciation of my friends. "What am I what?"

CeCe rolled her eyes as she wiped her fingers on her napkin, then started in on her own chips. "What are you doing for the silent auction on Saturday night?"

The big event for the weekend was a fundraiser for Jasper Days, set for next autumn. Once a month, the downtown business network sponsored a movie night with popcorn and a silent auction. The business owners in town took turns offering auction items. It had turned into quite a contest, with each owner trying to one-up the next.

"Not sure you'll be able to top the amount my basket got last month." CeCe brushed imaginary crumbs from her shoulder.

No denying that. CeCe's coffee baskets typically went for big bucks. In fact, I'd bid on a few myself.

My basket this month would include a five-class yoga pass with essential oils and some bath balls homemade by one of my students.

Cindy looked up from her phone. "Ooh, I bet that will smell good. I might have to bid on it."

I made a face. "What are you going to do with a yoga pass? You don't even pay for yoga."

"I'll pass it on to someone at the post."

CeCe gave one last pass over her plate, then took a swig of water. "Gotta run, ladies." She paused for dramatic effect as she slipped from the booth. "It's up to me to make sure Jasper is fully caffeinated to get through the afternoon!"

CeCe blew air kisses to each of us and speed-walked out of the diner as quickly as she had come,

After lunch, I joined Cindy and Josie on their walk back to the Sheriff's Department. As sheriff, Cindy kept getting stopped by passersby to ask her about one thing or another, so Josie and I walked on ahead. She took me back to the fingerprinting station.

"It's pretty mechanized now." Josie showed me how to place each of my fingers on the machine to get a good reading. She laughed as she had to wipe sweat off each finger before she lightly sprayed it with water.

"If you were any other person of interest, I'd say you were guilty of something, you're sweating so much," she teased. "Seriously, why are you nervous?"

I shrugged as much as I could and still keep my finger steady on the glass. "I think it's like when a police car pulls up behind you and you think you did something wrong. I know I haven't done anything, but this is an intimidating process."

Josie nodded in understanding, then handed me a bottle of hand sanitizer to wipe down my hands. "Don't worry about the investigation too much. You'll be fine and The Yoga Mat will be, too."

She gave me a wave and turned toward her desk. As I wandered out the door, feeling a little lost, I decided to go to the one place that always brought me peace: The Yoga Mat.

Stepping inside the studio doors, I paused and leaned against them, feeling the serenity that remained even after such a horrific event. Before anyone else came in, however, I wanted to refresh the studio. It seemed like the decent thing to do. Besides, someone had died here.

First, I jumped into a deep clean, dusting and wiping every surface then mopping and disinfecting. I took the rugs out the back door to shake them out. Finally I pulled out all of the studio's mats and vigorously wiped them down. Students are asked to wipe them down after each use, but I know they don't do it the way I would do it. The mats needed to be freshened up. After taking the covers off the bolsters and throwing them in a pile with the blankets to be washed, I loaded up everything in my arms and took it out the back door, throwing them in the back of my car.

Returning to the studio, I felt satisfied that it was physically clean. Next, I needed to clean the studio's energy. Though skeptics might laugh, I would remind them that when someone is angry or happy, you can feel it. That's energy and it's all around us. I didn't want any negative energy left in the room either by Patricia's death or the people who had come after her.

My singing bowl in hand, I walked purposefully from corner to corner, letting the ring from the bowl, which sounded sadder than usual today, fill the room, pushing out the negative vibrations and emptiness left by Patricia's death. Then I retraced my path, swinging the defuser with the scent of cypress lofting outward. Cypress is both uplifting and cleansing, both of which my own spirit and studio needed just then.

Finally, placing my mat in the middle of the room, I sat in meditation, bringing calm and peace back to the studio. Though I knew my yoga mentor would say death is a part of life, I didn't want its pallor hanging over my baby, my studio.

This was my dream. I'd discovered yoga in college and had practiced it off and on throughout my 20s and 30s, finally making the commitment to become a yoga instructor. Like many of my friends, I was feeling antsy as I passed forty, as if there was more to life than my job as a reporter for a Seattle newspaper. Besides, the newspaper business was in a steady decline, with newsroom layoffs nearly every quarter for the past couple of years.

My sister, the county sheriff, had been urging me to join her in Jasper. My parents had retired, splitting their time between Jasper and Arizona. My brother lived in a nearby town. A few years after my marriage had fallen apart, I decided to make another change and move to Jasper.

The first thing that had popped into my head was owning a yoga studio. I wasn't sure if I could make it work in a smallish town like Jasper, but with money I had invested after the divorce, I had a little time to figure it out.

As I opened my eyes and looked around the room, I sighed a breath of relief. The bad vibrations of yesterday's incident were gone and I was ready to have students join me again. I propped open the door and sent out a text to everyone on The Yoga Mat's mailing list that classes would resume at seven o'clock tomorrow morning. The Yoga Mat was back in business.

Chapter 6

During announcements before each class the next day, I briefly spoke about Patricia's death and told students I would update them if I heard anything about a memorial service.

During the 7 o'clock Morning Yoga class, I tiptoed around the class during savasana, just to make sure everyone was breathing. For the noon class, I stayed on my mat but sat up watchfully for any signs of disturbance.

By the five o'clock Vinyasa class, I breathed a bit easier. What were the odds that a student would die in my studio twice in one week?

During the five o'clock class, one student remained prone when class had ended. I hurried to his mat, alarm registering as I recognized another one of my regulars.

"Jason, can I help you?" I didn't even wait for a response, just put my head to his ear.

'Awhhfd!" Jason suddenly sat up, bumping our heads in the process.

"Mariah, what are you doing?"

"You-you-you're okay?" I stammered, then sat back on my heels as unbidden tears filled my eyes. "I'm sorry. I just, I just-"

Jason's eyes got big. "Oh, wait, you thought I was dead? Like Patricia?" He sat up straighter and pulled me in for a hug. "Ah, sweetie. That was a one-time thing." He pushed away and looked me in the eye. "It's not like it will ever happen again. Now, breathe. Please." He brushed the hair out of my face and smiled gently. "I'm sorry. I was just enjoying svasasana so much, I didn't want to move."

I took a deep breath and realized some of the rest of the class were still standing around.

I jumped up and started herding them toward the door. "Good class tonight, everyone! Sylvia, I noticed the effort you put into straightening out your lunge. I know you've been working on it. Way to go." Sylvia smiled shyly and stepped through the door to put on her shoes.

As the students filtered out, I noticed a shadowy figure hovering just inside the office door. Frowning, I stepped forward.

"Hello, can I help you?" I put on my most official voice.

A red-faced man with balding hair stepped out of the office. As I looked closer, I saw bloodshot eyes that didn't look exactly focused and dark circles underneath.

He hesitated. "I'm Todd McMillan."

I looked at him blankly. Was I supposed to know him?

"I'm Patricia's husband. *Was* Patricia's husband."

Oh.

I held out my hand to shake his, which felt damp and warm. "I'm so sorry for your loss, Mr. McMillan."

He nodded as he ran his hand over his head and looked around the studio.

"She loved this place," he said, looking doubtfully around like he wasn't sure why Patricia came here. He peered into the studio, then turned to gaze around the lobby area. Students slipped past him to get out.

"I'm glad. We loved having her here."

"You don't look like a yoga teacher."

I looked down at my slightly pudgy body and sighed. "I hear that a lot."

He nodded, peering at me from beneath bushy eyebrows, then hesitated, looking at the handful of students who remained in the studio and lobby. He leaned closer. Instinctively, I leaned away. "Where did it happen?" he whispered.

I bit my lip, then took him by the hand and gently led him into the studio, to the corner where Patricia had died on her mat.

"She was right about here," I told him, waving my hand in the general area where her mat had lain.

He stood for a long moment, eyes closed, breathing steady. When I thought he might have dozed off, he abruptly lifted his head.

"The police have been here?"

I nodded cautiously. "Of course."

"You know I'll have to file a wrongful death suit."

What? Startled, I jerked away from him. He continued without waiting for a more expansive response.

"She died here. I don't know what you did to her, but she died here." His face looked apologetic and his tone was thin, but his words cut like a blade.

"Mr. McMillan," I sputtered the words. "Mr. McMillan, I am sorry for your loss, but I think you should leave." I stalked through the studio toward the front doors and threw one open.

Jason slowly put on his shoes, obviously listening to the conversation, then stood up and walked a couple of steps toward me.

McMillan saw him and stopped. "We're not through," he said, then stumbled through the door.

I closed it behind him.

"Everything all right, Mariah?" Jason's eyes filled with concern.

I smiled at him and shrugged. "Patricia's husband. I'm sure he has some tough moments ahead of him."

Jason grimaced. "Just as long as he doesn't try to pass those on to you."

Jason wanted to wait for me to walk me to my car, just in case McMillan was waiting for me outside. I waved him off, assuring him I would be fine, a statement I wasn't sure I believed. He convinced me to let him go first and take a look around, just to be on the safe side. As I closed the door behind him, my eyes welled up with tears at his kindness. I felt exhausted. It felt nice to have someone looking out for me.

A few minutes later, Jason tapped at the door. "Mariah? It's me."

I opened the door and peeked out. I couldn't see much, but I heard Jason's deep voice. "The coast is clear. I think he's gone."

I opened the door all the way and gave Jason a quick hug, then closed the door. I hesitated, then turned the lock with a loud "click."

Chapter 7

The next morning, I got to the studio early, sending emails and text message reminders to private session clients, then preparing for the noon class. My cell buzzed while I was working out a particular hip opener sequence. I stopped when I saw who it was.

"Hey, sis."

"Mariah, we found Patricia's water bottle."

From the tone of her voice, that didn't sound like a good thing. "And…"

"Stormy McMcaster had it."

My brow furrowed on its own. Stormy? I didn't see a connection. Cindy correctly read my silence because she continued.

"Stormy McMaster? One of your new students? She was checked into the Jasper Medical Center with stomach cramps and nausea. Does that ring any bells?"

I thought a moment. "Those are the same symptoms that Patricia complained about the night she came to yoga class."

"Bingo. She brought the water bottle with her to the ER and kept crying about how karma was paying her back for taking a dead woman's water bottle, so one of the nurses called me to come over."

"And?" Irritation rose inside me as Cindy made this harder than it had to be.

"And Stormy told me how she saw Patricia's water bottle sitting there and figured she wasn't going to need it anymore, so she took it."

My mouth fell open. It was coming back to me now. Stormy was one of the newcomers to class that night. I suspected she'd been the one with the gum.

"She took a dead woman's water bottle?"

"Yep. She rinsed it out and refilled it with water, but whatever had been in it likely also caused Stormy's milder symptoms."

"Karma."

"Yeah, she actually got that part right, I think."

I heard the rueful smile in Cindy's voice that mirrored my own.

"She said she knew Patricia. What did you notice that night, sis?"

I pursed my lips as I tried to draw a picture of where their mats had been placed. Walking over to the corner of the studio, I spun slowly around. Patricia was here, Stormy and her friend Angela were in the next row by the wall with the lotus blossom on it. "They weren't right next to each other, if that's what you're asking," I finally said into the phone.

"But?" Cindy said. "I hear a 'but' in your voice."

I couldn't quite grasp the memory. "It seems like I heard Stormy greet Patricia. Yes, she did. Patricia was already here, putting down her mat, when I heard Stormy say something like, 'Why hello, Mrs. McMillan, how are you?' She sounded fakey nice, know what I mean? I didn't hear Patricia respond, but then Stormy asked about her daughter and said she heard she was seeing someone new in town. I don't know if Patricia responded, but she did move her mat away. Like she was trying to get away from Stormy."

"That girl's name seems to fit her."

"She snapped her gum during *savasana*. I know it was her."

"You're kidding. How rude!"

I silently thanked her for that. Really, only another yoga teacher would understand.

I snapped my fingers. "That's right, Patricia has a daughter. I remember now. Did you know she has a daughter?"

"Yes, Mariah, we're on top of that particular lead, thank you, and I know you're making a face at me."

I quickly resettled my facial features. "Oh, for Pete's sake. Stop that." I truly could not get away with anything with that woman.

"But you were."

Time to move on. "Are there any other children? Did she get along with her daughter?"

Cindy told me there were no other children, that the daughter was apparently a child with Husband Number Two, who lived in the Los Angeles area. As far as she knew, they got along.

"Do you think the daughter had anything to do with Patricia's death?"

"I don't know. Neil is following up on that angle."

"What about Stormy?"

"Not at this time, but we're not ruling anything out. Why do you keep asking questions about the case? Seriously, Mariah, we know how to do our jobs." Cindy's voice got a little edge to it, the way it does when she is irritated. "By the way, we are checking Patricia's water bottle for finger prints. Anything you want to tell me?"

"You mean, like the fact that she topped it off here before class?" Then another memory made me laugh. "Or that I practically played football with it one day and my fingerprints will be all over it?"

Cindy sighed. "That's what I was afraid of. You always did have a thing for shiny, sparkly things."

"Shall I run over to the hospital, steal the water bottle and wipe off my prints?"

Click. Cindy hung up on me. I would've done the same.

Stormy McMaster was in her early 20s, with languid energy rolling off of her when Angela brought her to The Yoga Mat. She was so busy looking into the studio to see who was there that she barely saw me and never really looked me in the eyes that whole night.

I hoped that the little bit of interaction would perhaps encourage her to talk to me more than she would talk to the detective. After a quick check of the clock, I locked the front door and bolted out the back. I had just enough time for a chat with Stormy before meeting Josie and CeCe for a late breakfast.

As my elevator stopped on the fourth floor of the hospital, Detective Neil Samuelson stepped out of a room down the hall and headed my way, fortunately looking down at that infernal notebook he carried.

With a gasp, I ducked around a corner and behind a cart sitting in the hallway. *Please, no one notice me crouching here!* I peeked around the cart in time to see Neil pause by the elevator, a stub of pencil in hand as he jotted something in his notebook. He took a breath and looked up at the ceiling, then cricked his neck from side to side. *For Pete's sake, this is the slowest elevator on the face of the Earth!*

A nurse's aide stopped just outside the room across from me and looked at me. My eyes widened and I shook my head putting my finger to my lips, silently begging him not to say anything. He hesitated, when at last, a cheerful "ding!" announced the elevator's arrival and the detective stepped into it, the doors whooshing quietly behind him.

Not that I'm paranoid, but I waited to make sure the elevator doors didn't pop back open, then I jumped up and dashed around the cart and down the hall to Stormy's room. First, a big breath, then I gently tapped on the door as I opened it.

Stormy lay on the bed, an arm flung over her eyes. She stirred when I softly said her name, then her face opened with recognition. "Mariah? The yoga teacher, right? What are you doing here?"

"I heard you were ill and wanted to stop by." I quietly entered the room, hoping to draw quiet and calm with me. "We like to think of ourselves as a community at The Yoga Mat and try to look after each other." This wasn't a lie, though I felt bad anyway. "How are you feeling?"

Stormy closed her eyes dramatically, then re-opened them. "I've felt better." She looked sheepish. "I don't suppose you heard."

I kept my face blank. It just didn't feel right acting surprised at what she was about to reveal to me. "Heard?"

She nodded, her eyes on the blanket that covered her. "I took Patricia McMillan's water bottle the night she died at yoga class. I guess there was some very toxic poison still in it." Her big brown eyes watered as she looked up at me. "I feel so stupid."

I gently patted her arm. "Happens to the best of us, I'm afraid. Why did you take it?"

She shrugged. "It seemed like easy revenge." She stuck her chin out and her look changed to one that more resembled defiance. "I used to be good friends with her daughter when we were in high school and Mrs. McMillan was always mean to me. She didn't think I was good enough to be hanging out with her precious child, like I was a bad influence or something."

I didn't have to fake surprise. This didn't sound like the Patricia I had known, however briefly. "What happened between you two the night at the studio? I thought I heard you talking to her."

"I told her I heard her daughter was seeing someone in town. Her daughter is gay. We've all known for years, but Mrs. McMillan has just never wanted to accept it. So when I saw her, I saw an opportunity to rub her face in it a little bit." Stormy cast her eyes downward again. "I'm not proud of that, by the way, not now, anyway."

Stormy shrugged. "Besides, it doesn't matter. She got the final revenge, right? I took her water bottle and then I got sick, too."

The door flew open and an aide entered with a tray. Stormy turned her attention to her and I knew I wouldn't get anything more today. I had just enough time to make it to CeCe's coffee shop to meet the girls. There wouldn't be time until later to mull over how this new information fit in the puzzle that was Patricia's life – and death.

Chapter 8

From across the table, Josie studied my food selections and shook her head. "Breakfast of yoga teachers? A mocha and a doughnut? You must still be in emotional eating mode."

I shrugged, picking up my sugar-encrusted snack, and broke it in half. I used it as a pointer as I gestured toward the mocha. "It's not that bad. I use almond milk, and a little sugar won't kill me. Remember, it's all about balance."

"I'm just saying I don't see you practicing *ahimsa* toward yourself here."

I glared at her over the table. "I wish I had never taught you about *ahimsa*." I shoved a bite of doughnut in my mouth. I talk about *ahimsa* with my students, particularly about practicing *ahimsa* toward themselves. I could deny it all I wanted, but Josie was right. I eyeballed the doughnut, then set it back on the plate.

Whenever we could, three or four of us met for meals or coffee during the day. Cindy was the only one of us married, so we tried to get together as much as possible.

CeCe interrupted us as she slid into the seat next to me. "Hey, gal pals. What's the latest on Patricia?"

She looked from me to Josie, then frowned at the chocolate frosting and sprinkles that had slipped from my doughnut to the table as well as coffee spills from Josie's apparently vigorous stirring.

"You guys have only been here five minutes. How did you make such a mess?"

Josie didn't hesitate. "She did it," she said, pointing across the table to me.

My mouth fell open. "Way to throw me under the bus, Jos. You know how she gets about messes."

"That's why you're under the back wheel, my friend. I'm not stupid."

CeCe shook her head at both of us, then stood up and went to the counter for a damp rag. She returned and quickly wiped down the table, then left to return the rag to its place on the counter.

"Spill it again," I whispered to Josie. "Quick! Before she gets back."

It was Josie's turn for her mouth to fall open. She hesitated, so I reached across the table and spilled more of her coffee on the table.

"Why my coffee? Why not yours?"

I shrugged and picked up my mocha. "You get free refills. This baby set me back a few bucks and no refills."

CeCe returned to the table and sat down again, stopping when she saw the fresh coffee spill. Josie didn't say a word, just pointed at me. Both of us bit our lips to keep from laughing.

CeCe pursed her lips as she took my napkin and wiped up the mess, shoving the napkin into her apron pocket.

"She's kind of mean, for a yoga teacher." Josie tried to get back on CeCe's good side.

CeCe sat up all prim and proper. "You know it's not nice to tease someone with a disability."

The three of us burst out laughing. "It's true, though," CeCe continued. "Obsessive Compulsive Disorder is a real thing."

"Then you probably went into the wrong business." I laughed again, throwing my arm around her shoulder. "But we will continue to support you here as long as the coffee keeps coming. Especially since Josie spilled half of hers."

"I di-" Josie started her denial, then stopped. "Never mind."

We laughed together and CeCe returned to the question she had asked. "So, what's up with Patricia's investigation?"

Josie looked hard at her coffee mug. "You know I can't talk about open cases."

"I'll give you more coffee."

"Stop trying to bribe me or I'll have to arrest you. I already get free refills."

"Well, Jos, do you have any suspects besides me?" I couldn't help but ask.

Josie shrugged. "We're checking alibis."

CeCe stared at Josie. "That's not very helpful for Mariah."

"What do you want? Of course, I know Mariah didn't kill anyone. But I still have to do my job."

I put my hand on CeCe's arm. "It's okay. I get it. It's just hard to feel like a suspect."

But even I knew I didn't have an alibi. I was in the room with Patricia when she died. *Ouch.*

"You're looking into the husband, right?" Josie raised her eyebrows, tilted her head to the side and stared at me. "Of course, you are. You always look at the spouse first." She offered a small smile.

I told the pair about my run-in with Patricia's husband the night before. They were sympathetic. "I don't think I handled it very well. Here's a man who clearly was in pain and I basically threw him out of the studio."

CeCe shrugged. "I would've done the same if someone came in here and did that. I would fight to keep it safe." She gestured around the room.

"However," I started, unsure how mad Josie would be if she knew I had talked to Stormy. They both looked at me expectantly. "I did talk to Stormy McMaster today."

CeCe looked puzzled. "Why would you talk to her?"

To her credit, Josie kept a stoic expression on her face. At least, I think she did. I was a little afraid to look at her as I filled CeCe in on the poisoned water bottle.

"No way!" CeCe shook her head, an incredulous smile playing at her lips. "Who takes a dead woman's water bottle, no matter how pretty it is? That takes guts, my friend."

"It's also not information that should be shared with the general public." I sneaked a peek at Josie now. Her eyebrows were one straight line. *Yikes.*

"I won't tell anyone, Josie, I promise." CeCe held up a finger and crossed her heart with it, then turned to me. "So do you think she killed Patricia?"

"I just said we're not supposed to talk about this information." Josie's voice went up in pitch and level.

I ignored her. "I don't really think so. She's irritating and obnoxious, but I don't think she's a killer."

CeCe sat back, nodding as she mulled over the new information. Then she sat up quickly. "On a completely different note, what do you think of the new detective?"

I reached over and held both of her cheeks in my hands and looked her square in the eyes. "He thinks I killed a woman in my own yoga studio. What do you suppose I think?"

CeCe gently released my hands and massaged her face. Apparently, I had pressed a bit too strongly. I patted her cheeks again.

She smiled. "That's true, but he's a cutie. And I can tell you that he likes to try new things. You know how you nearly always order a mocha?" I nodded. "He orders something different every time. He doesn't have a 'usual'." She used air quotes, then wiped the edges of the table as if checking for dirt. "I like that in a man."

"He just moved to town, Cee. He probably doesn't know what he likes yet."

"I know what he likes," Josie butted in as she moved to slip out of the booth. "He likes it when people don't blab information about suspects all over town. That's what he likes." She stood up and stalked out of the coffee shop.

CeCe and I followed her out the door with our eyes. Then CeCe sighed. "She didn't even leave a tip."

"We never leave a tip. We know the owner."

CeCe slipped out of the booth, and as I started to follow her, my cell phone buzzed.

It was Tabitha, my only part-time yoga instructor in addition to Cindy. "Mariah!" She breathed into the phone. "You'd better get over to the studio pronto!" I could tell Tabitha moved her head away from the phone and yelled at someone. "Hey, get away from there!"

Then the call ended.

I tripped on CeCe as I struggled to get out of the booth and ran for the door, CeCe on my heels. We raced past Josie down Main Street toward The Yoga Mat. "Josie, help!"

I heard her start to run behind me. Even from three blocks away I could see commotion and a growing crowd in front of the studio. *My studio.*

Pushing past the people, I halted in my tracks. Hand-made posters reading "Killer Yoga" and "Corpse Pose is Real" were propped up around The Yoga Mat. In the center of the chaos, Todd McMillan walked back and forth in front of the studio, a sign in his hand that read "Killers inside. Beware!"

When he saw me, McMillan stopped and pointed a beefy finger in my direction. "There she is! She killed my wife!"

Chapter 9

I pushed past McMillan into the studio, CeCe on my heels. Josie stopped to talk with McMillan. He started to argue with her until she pulled out first her badge and then apparently a list of the laws he was violating at that moment. She walked several paces away from the studio and motioned to McMillan to join her. When he refused, she flipped on her shoulder headset and spoke into it, then came and stood between McMillan and the studio.

A few minutes later, reinforcements showed up, taking McMillan by the hands and placing him in a deputy's car. His face got redder and redder as they drove away, leaving his posters lying on the sidewalk. Josie picked them up and tossed them into the nearest public trash bin, then dispersed the crowd and came inside.

"He's gone for now, but no doubt he will be back." Her voice was matter of fact acknowledging she'd been through this kind of thing before, some of the "imperfect humanness" that Detective Samuelson had talked about.

"How can he protest me when he doesn't even know what the truth is?"

Josie shrugged. "People believe what they want to believe, especially if they're grieving. You can get a restraining order if you'd like that could keep him farther away from the studio."

I hesitated, then shook my head, releasing a breath I didn't realized I'd been holding. "Not yet. *Ahimsa*. Let me practice non-violence toward him and see if things settle down."

Josie looked skeptical but nodded, then checked her watch. "Okay, I have to get to the station. Holler if you need me."

Just as the door was closing, it swung open again. Detective Neil Samuelson filled the doorway.

"Ms. Stevens, we need to talk."

I laughed nervously so that it came out as more of a bark. "Oh, it's back to Ms. Stevens, is it? That can't be good."

He looked at CeCe and then at me.

"I should go." CeCe picked up her purse.

"No, you can stay," I said.

"She probably should go," the detective chimed in.

"Anything you have to say to me, you can say in front of her." I challenged him with my eyes.

He looked from CeCe to me and back again, then nodded. CeCe took her purse off her shoulder and set it back down.

The detective motioned us to sit. "Patricia McMillan had a new will drawn up recently. Guess who got a whole boatload of her money?"

I looked at CeCe and we both shrugged. "I didn't know her well enough to begin to guess at that, Detective."

He leaned toward me and looked at me hard. "You, Ms. Stevens. She left it to you. $25,000."

All the air rushed out of my lungs as I gasped. "What? How is that possible? She barely knew me."

"She left it to you for The Yoga Mat. Apparently, it changed her life or something."

"You knew. That's why you acted all suspicious about me earlier. You knew she had changed her will."

The detective seemed flustered as he ran his fingers through his hair. He watched me carefully. "Her family had suspected it. We read the will ourselves a short time ago. I'm not going to lie, this looks bad for you."

I nodded, wrapping my arms around myself. He stood up to leave. "You are now officially a suspect, Ms. Stevens. Don't leave town."

As soon as the door closed softly behind him, CeCe and I locked eyes.

"Now will you help me?"

"What happened to *ahimsa*?"

"I can still practice non-violence while I search for the killer. I did a lot of research when I worked for newspapers, and, clearly, the sheriff's office is not moving fast enough."

"But that's your sister and best friend you're talking about."

"I know." I locked eyes with her. "So we're not going to tell them."

Later that day, after a full slate of classes and private sessions, I finally closed the door on the studio and walked along Main Street to meet CeCe for dinner. We had settled into our booth at the diner on the other end of Main Street from the coffee shop. CeCe stretched her arms up over her head. I could tell she was starting to wind down from work. She sipped a glass of wine. I sipped the diner coffee. It wasn't as good as CeCe's and she knew it.

CeCe got us started. "What do we really know about Patricia, other than she did yoga? Where did she work before she retired? Did she put it on her yoga form?"

"No, I don't care how they make money as long as they bring it to me."

"You're awfully cold-hearted for a yoga teacher."

"I've come to accept it." I took a sip of coffee. "But it does make me wonder where *did* she get all her money?"

CeCe thought about it, her hand playing with the stem of the wine glass. "Husbands."

"Seriously?"

She nodded. "She was on Husband Number Four or Five, Mariah. All of them had a lot of money and she got a bunch when they divorced. I hear she had a great lawyer."

"Even Todd? He doesn't look like he comes from money." CeCe raised her eyebrows. "Not that I'm saying he looks like trailer trash or anything. But-"

"What's wrong with trailer trash?" CeCe sat up a little straighter and peered at me across the table. "I grew up in a trailer. Lots of 'em. They were affordable and didn't have a yard, so my mom, a single mom, by the way, loved them."

I reached across the table and took CeCe's hand. "I'm so sorry. I didn't mean to say trailer trash. I just meant, well, his clothes were not luxury brands and they didn't hang on him very well."

"Not that you noticed."

"I notice things about people who come into my business." I smiled, then wrinkled my brow again. "He didn't seem like he came from money, that's all."

CeCe nodded. "You're not wrong. From what I hear, Todd McMillan won a big lottery prize several years ago. Patricia married him shortly after that and she's the one that got him to invest his money. He's set for life, thanks to Patricia."

That was interesting to hear. Perhaps McMillan had found out Patricia was going to divorce him and decided to turn the tables on her instead.

CeCe dug in her purse, then slapped a pad of paper and a pen on the table.

"Notes," she said in response to my raised eyebrow. "We need to make a list of suspects."

"Okay. Let's do this." I pumped my fists.

CeCe stared at me, her pen poised over the paper. "And?"

"It's Todd McMillan."

The pen dropped in CeCe's hand. "Seriously?"

"Yes, I really think it is."

She stared at me pointedly.

I felt myself reverting to my reporter days. I would go all out to get a story. I hated the police beat, though I had worked it for a few years. I once had to interview a mother in the hospital about her son who had died in the same car crash that put her there. Another time, I wrote about people who had been displaced by a fire. The news was often sad. I had switched to the investigative team, where people did bad things but didn't die or get maimed. I felt myself tap into those skills, so I reached across the table and took the pad from CeCe.

She shrugged as I wrote Todd McMillan on the pad.

"I'm putting a star next to his name," I muttered out loud. "I think he did it."

She cocked an eye at me and pulled the pad back across the table. "Were you an unbiased reporter at all?"

I sighed. Maybe CeCe was right. Todd McMillan had accused me of killing his wife and now apparently he was trying to kill my business in return. So perhaps, just maybe, as my mother liked to say, I had a bone to pick with him. But I sat back in my seat, took a deep breath and tried to open my mind to other possibilities. CeCe nodded in approval as she tapped her chin with her finger.

I lasted about 15 seconds.

"Nope, it's him."

CeCe threw up her arms in frustration, then leaned on the table to stare at me. "Mariah, get a grip. This is not all about you. You're not the one who died on that mat. Now, please, who else could it be?"

"Okay, look," I leaned toward her. "The police always start with the spouse. It just makes sense because they're the closest to the victim and they have the most to lose. Todd had opportunity and motive. and even he could figure out where to get poison."

I crossed my arms and sucked in my lower lip. CeCe began to nod slowly.

"I see your point. Let's just brainstorm and see if any other suspects show up."

Instinctively, I closed my eyes tightly and opened my mouth wide. I had started doing that when I first began my yoga practice several years ago, once I realized I carried tension in my jaw. It helped. The subsequent breath also helped to bring me back to the café and out of my ever-so-busy head. I considered what I knew about Patricia, then snapped my fingers.

"Stormy McMaster!" CeCe's head jerked up as she looked at me.

"You said at breakfast you didn't think it was her."

In frustration, CeCe reached across the table and grabbed the back the notepad.

I shrugged. "I figure we need to brainstorm. It could be her."

CeCe frowned. "I don't see how. Clearly, it has to be someone who was close to her and was able to poison her."

I tapped the paper and CeCe reluctantly wrote down "Stormy." She looked up at me. "Who else?"

I shrugged, then an idea came to me. Patricia had died during the Safety Blanket fund-raiser. Maybe someone at the nonprofit had a problem with her? I suggested as much to CeCe. Her brow furrowed.

"I hate the idea that it would be some with a group that is trying to help moms and babies."

"Me, too, but we need to look at them. I'll try to talk to Jennifer tomorrow."

CeCe and I sat in silence for a few moments.

"What about her sister?" I thought out loud. "Melinda was the one who brought her to The Yoga Mat in the first place. She said Patricia was having a tough time with retirement and that yoga was just the thing to help her."

I sat back smiling, pleased with myself for coming up with another suspect. "Oh wait," I thought out loud. "No, I don't think she's really a suspect. She was trying to help her sister."

"Maybe not," CeCe agreed. "But maybe she can add someone to our list?" She started to write down Melinda's name. "Write a sec. Do you mean Melinda Jacobs? She's Patricia's sister?"

"You look surprised. Do you know her?"

CeCe made a face and started to respond, but just then our meals were served. CeCe went for the country fried steak and eggs, this being a diner after all. I had a Southwestern salad with black beans.

Once we had settled into our respective meals, CeCe answered the question. "Melinda Jacobs is a pain in the butt."

I smiled as I chewed, waiting for her to continue.

"She comes into the shop quite a bit and always wants her latte at such-and-such degrees because she read about it in some magazine article. So we do it just the way she wants it for a few days. Then the next time she comes in, she yells at us about doing the way she had asked before because she has since decided that the article was wrong."

I nodded over my salad. I had noticed the Melinda could be particular at times, but at the studio, she kept a low profile. She had been coming almost since the studio opened and I counted her as a loyal regular. After all, she had bought a six-month pass. However, since Patricia began attending classes, Melinda had not come as often and rarely came to the same classes as her sister. It hadn't concerned me; I figured she would be back at some point. Sometimes people try not to get in each other's way.

"She went on and on about those damn gophers in her yard, how their bodily functions – and she didn't put it quite so nicely – got all over her yard and into her garden."

"She had gophers in town?"

CeCe shrugged. "You know that neighborhood on the edge of downtown, pushed back into the hill a ways? That's where she lives."

I wasn't familiar with that part of town. Even though Jasper wasn't large, pockets remained that I had yet to explore.

"Let's put her on the list of people to talk to. She might be able to help us out."

CeCe made a face. "If she starts talking about gophers again, I will stick a pen in my eye."

"Ballpoint? I'll make sure I have one with me."

CeCe picked up a big chunk of chicken-fried steak from her plate and waved it in front of my nose. "Sure you don't miss it?"

"Now you're just being mean."

Once in a while, particularly at the diner, I could be tempted by a basket of fried shrimp with ranch dressing. I'm not proud of it, but some habits die hard.

Tonight, however, I was eating healthy after consuming sugar and salt in the days immediately after Patricia's death. I didn't like to think I was an emotional eater, but the evidence said differently.

The little bell over the diner's doorway dinged. I glanced up to see who had come in, then quickly looked back at my plate.

Detective Samuelson stood in the doorway. He greeted the waitress, then headed over to the counter to sit down, turning the coffee cup right side up on the saucer. He picked up the menu, then held it to his face to cover a yawn. The server behind the counter appeared with a pot of coffee, greeting the detective and filling his cup. They chatted, then the detective's eyes went back to the menu, then flickered over to where CeCe and I were sitting just in time to see both of us watching him.

"Good evening, ladies."

CeCe greeted him in return, but I just glared at him, then dug back into my food.

CeCe kicked me under the table and hissed at me. "Be civil."

"I won't. He thinks I killed someone." I didn't bother to lower my voice to match hers. Let the detective hear me. "Clearly he has no idea what he's doing. We'll probably figure out who the killer is before he does."

Samuelson sighed and stepped down from the counter, coming toward us. He stopped and squatted down next to our table, turning to look me in the eyes. "Bad-mouthing me in front of other citizens will not help your case, Ms. Stevens. I understand you're angry. I'd like you to understand I am just following the evidence. If it leads to you, I will not hesitate to arrest you. Please don't make me arrest you sooner for slandering an officer or interfering with an official investigation."

I sat back in my chair, pretty sure he was bluffing. "I have First Amendment rights. You can't do that."

"Watch me."

Our eyes held, then he tipped his head to me and stood up, walking slowly back to his seat. "I'll take my food to go, please," he told the waiter.

Within a few moments, he and his food were gone. CeCe watched me silently, then turned her attention back to her food. I didn't feel good about what I'd said, but no way was I going to let him railroad me in Patricia's death.

Chapter 10

CeCe stared at the GPS on her phone. She shook her head for the umpteenth time. "I still don't like this."

"We're not doing anything wrong. We're just going to talk to Melinda to find out more about Patricia. You know her better than I do."

CeCe sighed again. "I didn't say I liked her. She comes into the shop a lot – and that is one woman who does not need more caffeine."

CeCe's phone guided them toward Melinda's neighborhood. As they turned off the main road onto a side street, a large rusted eyesore of a building sitting on the far end of a large parking lot glared in the sun.

"What is that place?" I asked, nodding toward the building while keeping my eyes on the road.

"That's the Old Gym." CeCe looked up from her cell phone to appraise the building. "The City Council is trying to decide what to do with it, but if they don't agree soon, it will just be torn down. Turn left up here."

After a few more turns, we pulled up in front of Melinda Jacob's house and walked carefully to the front porch.

Melinda Jacobs looked like a hopped-up version of Patricia, if Patricia had been doing meth. Thin, gaunt even, with dark circles under her red-rimmed eyes and her face drawn back, Melinda flung open the door before the bell had barely finished ringing. CeCe and I stepped back in surprise.

She greeted us hesitantly and frowned through the screen door. "What can I do for you?"

She didn't open the screen door, so we just started talking over each other.

"We came to offer our condolences," Cecelia started.

"We were so sorry to hear about Patricia." I mentally kicked myself that it was the best I could come up with. Melinda seemed to agree.

"Heard about her?" I could swear she sneered. "She died in your studio. You were there."

"I-I-I know," I stammered, looking frantically at CeCe, who shrugged back at me. "I just, well, I wanted to express my condolences, and when I tried to express them to Patricia's husband, he wasn't very receptive."

Melinda's tone changed abruptly as she rolled her eyes and pushed open the door. "That man doesn't have an ounce of sense or good grace."

I turned to CeCe. "You were right. We should have come to Melinda directly." I turned back to Melinda as we entered the house. "I am so glad to hear you say that. I thought it was just me who thought that way."

She shook her head as she led us into a seating area off what appeared to be a living room. "Todd can be crude sometimes, but he's not a bad guy. Patty probably drove him to drink more than he used to. He was not her type at all. I still cannot fathom why she decided to marry him. I tried to talk her out of it, but clearly that didn't work."

As we sat down, CeCe took both of Melinda's hands and looked deeply at her. "It's still so hard to believe she's gone. She was just in the shop the day she passed. She spoke of you then. You were so special to her."

Melinda awkwardly removed her hands from CeCe's and clenched them in her lap. She looked at her hands for a moment in silence. Tears began to trickle down her face and she gasped a little as she tried to talk. CeCe reached over to pick up a broach from the coffee table and held it up.

"Patricia had this with her in the shop just the other day. She couldn't wait to give it to you."

Melinda snatched the pin away and began twisting it in her hands.

"I found this on her desk in a little box with my name on it."
She let the broach lie in her hand. "She was the best big sister, always
so thoughtful. I don't know what I'll do without her." Melinda swiped
at her face with a tissue with one hand, clutching the pin with the
other.

"Tell us about Patricia." CeCe patted her leg and spoke calmly.
Apparently, the yoga was working for my caffeinated friend.

Melinda attempted a watery smile. "She always encouraged me
to do my best and was always trying to find me a husband, which is
funny since she had so many." Her tears slowed and her forehead
wrinkled. "She would always get bored of her husbands once they had
been married a few years. She was even starting to talk about dumping
Todd and I thought she loved him most of all. She was so fickle."

CeCe laughed. "That's a word you don't hear very often."

"It's true, though." Melinda turned toward CeCe and took her
hand. "She would start finding the tiniest things wrong with her
husbands and then start picking at them. Before I knew it, another
marriage would just fall apart and Patricia would always be so 'poor
me, poor me'. I tried and tried to get her to go to therapy, but she
wouldn't go." She turned and looked pointedly at me. "I really thought
yoga was helping her be more grounded since she retired."

"What exactly did Patricia retire from?"

A smile crossed Melinda's face. "She was in IT, just like me. In fact, she's the one who pushed me toward computers back when fewer women were in the field."

"IT, huh?"

Melinda laughed and leaned in conspiratorially. "Sure, what better way to spend all day at social media sites than being an IT manager?" She laughed again. "Not really. But Patricia loved all things computer. She was a wiz at database management."

I nodded like I knew what that was, so Melinda continued. "Her company was beginning to downsize and offered her a hefty retirement package, so she took it."

Melinda abruptly stood up and stepped away from the couch, rubbing her hands down her legs, her back to us. "I wish I had been in town when it happened. I keep thinking that perhaps I could have helped. It's silly, I know."

"Where were you?" I asked as gently as I could.

"I was at a conference all week in San Jose. I took the train. I hate to drive in the city, so I usually go by train. I just came back when I heard about my sister."

I scooted in to sit next to CeCe. "Melinda, the police seem to suspect foul play. We've been trying to help them figure it out, you know, with my sister being sheriff and all. Do you have any ideas who might want your sister dead?"

Melinda turned and stared at me, so I abruptly tried to backpedal. "It might be too soon to talk about this, of course. We can always come another time."

She covered her mouth with her hand. "I've been struggling with this ever since the Sherriff's Office told us they suspected someone had murdered her. Who would do sch a thing? Who would kill Patty?"

The tears started to flow again as CeCe and I exchanged a glance. We stood up, and I gave Melinda a hug. "We'll let you have some time. Call us if you need anything."

Melinda walked us to the door and thanked us for coming.

CeCe shot me a glance as we pulled away from the curb in front of Melinda's house. "For a yoga teacher, you lie way too easily."

"I teach yoga. I'm not the clergy."

"Well, that makes it okay." I was pretty sure CeCe was being sarcastic, so I rolled my eyes.

I felt defensive, and I'm sure it was because I did not feel great about lying to Melinda. Her sister was dead, and we'd just pumped her for information. Probably information the detectives already had, but what was done was done.

"I knew it was that slime ball."

"Again, you're a yoga teacher?"

"Shut up! I'm trying to think out loud here. He was pushy and tried to intimidate me and ruin my business. I'm allowed to be mad at him."

"And think he killed someone?"

"Yes, and think he killed someone."

I gunned the car down the street to emphasize my point.

Chapter 11

CeCe and I had a lot to do before we could get back to work. We had decided to interview both Patricia's sister and daughter before we had to be back at our respective businesses.

"Never mind. Next?"

CeCe typed Patricia's daughter's address into the phone.

I tried to remember what Patricia had said about her daughter. She had mentioned her daughter would be pleased that she was doing yoga, but other than that, Patricia had not talked about her daughter much, which I thought in retrospect was odd.

I didn't have children, so I couldn't say for sure, but Cindy and CeCe both talked about what their kids were doing. Sometimes way more than I wanted to hear. Not that the roommate troubles of CeCe's college-aged son weren't fascinating, but, well, they actually weren't interesting at all.

We didn't want to talk to Patricia's daughter while Todd was in the vicinity, so we stopped for coffee at CeCe's, then camped out in front of Patricia's neighbor's home while we waited.

"I'm missing the mid-morning rush." CeCe fumed for at least the twelfth time.

"Thank you for doing this with me. It means so much to me and to my business." I kept looking out the window at the house kitty-corner across the street, but I could see CeCe eye me suspiciously.

"You're playing me." Her tone was matter-of-fact. And she wasn't wrong.

"No, I'm not. I do appreciate it. I am trying to save my business. I also know you don't like the morning rush anyway."

She punched me on the arm. I looked at her laughing. "What are you, twelve?"

She punched me again. I might bruise from that one, so I pulled my arm away.

"Thanks for the coffee, by the way. No one makes it better." I lifted my non-dairy mocha in a sincere salute. It was still warm.

"Shut up."

I laughed again. There was nothing I could say now that would appease her. But I was glad she had agreed to come with me.

A tap on my window right behind my ear made me jump so high I nearly spilled my drink.

I turned to look into the blue eyes of Detective Neil Samuelson. He made the old-fashioned motion to roll down my window. I pretended for a moment not to understand. He frowned at me.

I pressed the button to lower the window. "You're showing your age, Detective. No one actually rolls a window up or down anymore."

He made a face at me that was so charming it caught me off guard and I found myself laughing and staring into those sparkling blue eyes.

He broke the spell, though, and reminded me that I was mad at him. "Interesting place for a coffee break, ladies."

CeCe and I just looked at each other. I lifted the cup for him to see. "CeCe really does make the best coffee."

"Oh, I agree," he smiled. "I'm working on one in my car right now. So what exactly are *you* doing here?"

CeCe leaned around me so she could see him more clearly. "It's not against the law to sip our coffee on any street in the city, detective."

He nodded. "True, but it *is* against the law to interfere with an official law enforcement investigation."

I studied my coffee in the silence that followed. Finally, I looked up at him.

"Look, Todd McMillan keeps disrupting my business by telling people I killed Patricia. You know that's not the truth. I have to clear my name. I can't lose my business." I nodded over to CeCe. "We thought if we talked to Patricia's daughter, Allison, she might tell us more than if you talked to her, since we actually knew her mom."

He nodded back at me. "That might be true. I've spoken to her already and she wasn't all that forthcoming with information. That's why I'm here to talk with her again, hopefully without her stepdad around."

Just then, Neil's eyes widened. I followed his gaze to see the garage at Patricia's house going up. Neil pulled on the backdoor handle. "Let me in." His voice was urgent as he crouched down by the door.

"Let us go in with you to talk to Allison."

"No."

I started to raise the window as I watched Todd McMillan's car backing out of the driveway, nearing the street.

"Okay, okay, let me in."

I unlocked the door and Neil slid into the back seat. "Get your heads down." We did as he said and heard McMillan's car pass by. We waited until he was at the end of the street before lifting our heads.

Neil started to open the back door, but I hit the child-proof lock.

"Mariah, don't be childish. Let me out."

"You said we could go in with you."

Our eyes met in the rearview mirror. Finally, he sighed. "Okay, you can come, but let me do the talking."

I unlocked his door, and the three of us stepped out of the car, trooping together up the driveway of Patricia's well-kept home. The garden was immaculate, with raised flower beds and crisp edges.

After the detective rang the bell, the three of us waited in silence, CeCe and I swapping glances and avoiding Neil's eyes. Just as he reached for the bell again, steps sounded inside and the door opened a few inches.

"Yes?" A quiet voice emanated from the darkness inside.

The detective stepped forward and peered inside. "Miss Harris? It's Detective Samuelson. We spoke a couple of days ago. I wonder if you have time to answer a few more questions."

"Of course, detective." She pushed the door open. Samuelson took the handle and stepped back to let us enter first. Allison backed up when she saw us.

I had not seen her up close before. Her eyes and nose reminded me of Patricia, but where Patricia had some middle-age spread, Allison was slender. Where Patricia's hair had been curly, Allison's was thick and long, probably beautiful under better circumstances but now hanging limply to the sides of her face. With both hands, she pushed back her hair, holding it there for a moment as she studied us. Dark circles ringed her eyes and she blinked a few times as if trying to clear her vision.

CeCe stepped forward first and introduced us. "We were friends of your mom's and wanted to come by and offer our condolences when we ran into the detective outside."

Allison nodded slightly but kept staring at me. I took her by the hand and spoke quietly to her. "Your mom was at my yoga studio when she passed. I want you to know she was peaceful."

She jerked her hand away from mine. "Todd said you had something to do with her death. Why else would she have died there?"

I shook my head softly from side to side, placing my hand over my heart as I tend to do when I'm feeling passionate. "Your stepfather is mistaken. We had nothing but love and respect for Patricia at The Yoga Mat. I'm so very sorry for your loss."

Neil cleared his throat. "Miss McMillan, perhaps you and I can talk first and then you can conclude your meeting with these ladies."

Allison looked back at him, then at us and nodded. She turned on her heel, shuffling into the living room behind her. She flopped on the couch without offering us a seat. We took one anyway.

"When we spoke earlier, you said you were at the university when your mother died?" The detective spoke gently but firmly.

Allison nodded, her hands resting on her knees. She lifted her eyes and held his gaze.

"When I called your school, your math professor said you were absent that day."

Allison shrugged. "He made a mistake. I make it a point not to miss classes. I'm an A student, detective."

"I know. I checked your transcript."

Allison's eyes narrowed, but she said nothing.

"You missed a quiz that day." Her eyes shot up to his face and he pressed on. "You don't remember a quiz?"

Her tongue started playing with the inside of her mouth, apparently a nervous habit, then she shook her head and smiled ruefully. "I guess I forgot we had a quiz that day."

"Where were you, since you clearly weren't in class?"

She shrugged and stared at the floor. "I guess I overslept for class."

Neil looked like he didn't believe her. She met his gaze, clearly – at least to me – challenging him to argue with her. I saw an opening, so I took it.

"Happens all the time to college kids," I murmured to myself and turned to CeCe. "Your son oversleeps sometimes, doesn't he?"

She started to shake her head, but I elbowed her in the ribs. "Ouch! Yes, of course, every college student sleeps through a class sometimes. I did it myself when I was in college."

Neil turned to stare at us, his face impassive. When he thought Allison couldn't see his face, he made his eyes big. Even I could read the question: *What the heck are you doing?*

I wanted to reassure, but instead I pressed forward. "I think Allison is probably exhausted right now, detective. Perhaps it's time to let her relax."

CeCe jumped up. "Let me make you some tea, sweetie." She didn't wait for a response, just hurried through a door that looked like it went to the kitchen. Allison stayed where she was, now looking at her hands clenched in her lap.

Samuelson stood up and put his notebook in his pocket. He grasped my arm and pulled me up with him. "Miss Harris, I'll be in touch. Mariah, walk me out." It wasn't a question. As soon as we were next to the door, I wrenched myself from his grasp.

"That kind of hurt."

He had the good grace to pause. "Sorry. What are you doing? I was questioning her."

"It was clear she was not going to answer any more of your questions," I hissed at him. "Let CeCe and me talk to her. I'll call you as soon as we're done, I promise."

"You're on my suspect list. I can't leave you alone with her."

"CeCe is here. She's not a suspect."

He grunted in frustration but reached for the door and let himself out, closing the door probably louder than he could have.

I bustled back into the living room to find CeCe fussing over Allison. Tea and toast already sat on the coffee table in front of Allison. CeCe is a wiz at tea and toast.

"I was just trying to get Allison to eat a little. It's hard when your mind isn't on food."

Allison dutifully took a couple of bites of toast, washing them down with the tea. We sat quietly and watched her for several long and what felt to me like awkward moments.

Finally, she stopped and looked at me. "Thank you for getting rid of that police officer."

"He's a sheriff's detective."

"Whatever. Thank you."

"You looked like you needed a break."

She gave me a little smile.

"You didn't really oversleep for your quiz, did you?"

She sighed, her shoulders drooping. Then she looked at me and silently shook her head.

"Where were you?"

Tightening her clasped hands around the tea cup was the only sign she gave that she had even heard me. CeCe jumped in.

"You have to realize, Allison, that if you don't tell us, we will look at your phone records to find out where you were."

Allison's head jerked up. "You can do that?"

CeCe nodded matter-of-factly. Still Allison didn't speak.

After several long months, I gently reached over and rubbed her back. "They say the truth will set you free, Allison. In my experience with yoga, I've found that to be true."

She looked at me and smiled wearily, tears coming to her eyes. "You told that to my mom, didn't you? She came home one night from yoga class and told me about it. It changed her life." She grimaced and peered into her tea cup. "Mine, not so much."

I frowned, puzzled. "What do you mean, sweetie?"

She gave a short laugh. "My mom was going on and on about how the truth would set her free."

CeCe and I exchanged a look over Allison's head. She picked up the thread. "What did your mother mean by that, that the truth would set her free?"

Allison smiled a small smile and rolled her eyes. "I think she was planning on getting rid of husband number five."

"Todd?"

"Really?"

CeCe and I spoke at the same time. Allison just nodded. I felt like we were pulling the proverbial teeth, but I wanted her to keep talking.

Allison sipped her tea, relaxing into the sofa. Her shoulders relaxed and she yawned, covering her mouth and apologizing. At least Patricia had taught her good manners.

"She and Todd used to have a lot of fun together, but they didn't spend much time together anymore. Todd wasn't around a lot, usually at a bar or drunk in the den, and then Mom found yoga."

I waited for the "and—," but Allison paused to sip her tea.

"That's pretty much all I know about it. See, she was so into the 'truth will set you free' mode that I finally told her my truth – and she blew up at me."

"Which is?"

"I've been dating a woman. Here in Jasper. That's where I was when she died, just across town."

She stared at her cup as if a portal would open up and swallow her.

"You mom wasn't happy that you had found someone?"

She shook her head. "My girlfriend is a resident at the hospital, so I even joked about it. 'Look, Mom, even you should appreciate that I might marry a doctor,' but she was so against it. Thank goodness, Aunt Mel was on my side. She said Mom would come around, just give her time." Her eyes welled with tears again and she reached for a tissue. "But she ran out of time."

CeCe took Allison's face and turned it to look her straight in the eye. "Allison, your aunt was right. Your mom loved you. She made a mistake by not accepting your girlfriend, but there's no doubt in my mind she loved you. We moms aren't perfect, but we love our kids."

Tears trickled out of Allison's eyes and down her cheek.

"Thank you for telling us, sweetie." CeCe wiped her tears and hugged her, rocking her gently on the couch for a long moment.

"Allison, would your girlfriend say you were with her?"

She lifted her head to look at me. "I guess, but I don't want to out her. She doesn't advertise that she's gay."

I remembered what Stormy McMaster had said about Allison. "Did your mom know Stormy McMaster?"

Allison looked at me in surprise. "Stormy? Sure, from when we were kids. Oh, and she did tell me that Stormy had applied for a job with her company, but she didn't get it."

"Why didn't she?"

Allison shrugged. "Mom didn't like her much. Said she was a bad influence on me and partied too much." She gave a slight smile at the memory. "It .was probably the other way around, though. I think I was the bad influence."

"Do you know anyone else who might have wanted to kill your mother?" I asked gently, stroking her arm.

She stared into the cup some more, then finally it down on the coffee table in front of her and turned to look at me and shrugged. "Seems like everyone was mad at her right now – me, Todd, Aunt Melanie. I've even wondered if she did it to herself. She didn't like having people mad at her."

"Why was Melanie mad at her?" CeCe picked up the empty cup and crumb-stained saucer.

"She got mad every time Mom got divorced, called her a gold digger and all that." Her eyes looked anxious. "But she wasn't a gold digger. I think she just got tired of men after a while. Sometimes, I thought Aunt Mel was mad at her all the time anyway because of what happened to Grandma and Grandpa."

CeCe and I exchanged a puzzled look, then waited for Allison to continue. She didn't, so I broke first and prompted her. "What happened to them?"

"They died in a car crash on their way to help Mom when she was going through Divorce Number Two, no wait, Three, yeah, Divorce Number Three. Aunt Mel always blamed Mom for that."

With that statement, as if she had no more to give, Allison leaned her head on the back of the couch. As I gently guided Allison onto her side, tucking a pillow under her head, CeCe showed up at my side with an afghan.

"I found this tossed over a chair," she whispered. I smiled sadly back at her, then helped her tuck in Allison. CeCe bent over and swiftly gave her a kiss on the forehead. Allison smiled slightly and briefly.

We picked up our purses, checked that the front door was locked and closed it behind us.

"Poor kid." CeCe mused as we walked down the driveway, tucking her arm in mine.

"We think she's a poor kid," I corrected CeCe. "But she might be a killer."

CeCe scoffed. "She's no killer. You felt her energy. I know you did. I saw you watching her."

I nodded slowly. Sadness had enveloped Allison, but was it because her mother was killed or because she killed her mother?

"Could we really have checked her phone records?" That question had been bothering me since CeCe had suggested it.

"I certainly hope so," she said, looping her arm in mind. "What good is it to have a sister who is sheriff if we can't check someone's cell phone log?"

Hard to argue with that

Chapter 12

Detective Samuelson sat on the curb next to my car. His face was grim as he stood and brushed off his trousers.

I frowned at him. "I told you I would call you when we were done. You didn't believe me?"

"Let's just say I was skeptical. What did you learn?"

I looked up at Patricia's house just in time to see the curtain move in the front room. Was Allison watching us? I thought she had gone right to sleep. I waved him away. I didn't want Allison to know we were about to betray her confidence.

"Nothing, okay, we learned nothing, and please act like we're not giving you anything just in case she is watching from the window."

Neil stared at me, then threw up his hands and stalked away. I exhaled in relief as I stepped into the car.

CeCe watched me carefully as I turned the key in the ignition. "We are going to tell him what we learned, right?"

"Oh yeah," I agreed. "Could you text him to meet us at your shop? I am not nearly caffeinated enough."

CeCe pulled out her phone and sent the text.

"You believe her, don't you?"

I nodded slowly. "In this day and age, why would she lie about being gay? That seems pointless. But it doesn't sound like Patricia took it very well."

"She was pretty old school. I remember she came in, gosh, I think it was the day she died or the day before and she showed me that vintage pin she got for her sister. It struck me as rather old-fashioned, but she loved it. She couldn't wait to give it to Melinda."

"I'm glad Melinda found it."

CeCe nodded in agreement. We drove back to the coffee shop in silence, each processing our interviews.

When we got to the coffee shop, CeCe slipped behind the counter and pulled an apron over her head. Bustling up to the line, she expertly tied it behind her back and swiftly took the next order. Her head barista, Paul, glanced at her and kept foaming the milk as he filled her in on the mid-morning rush. They had been working together for a couple of years now and were a well-oiled machine.

I placed my order and found a table near a window, barely looping my purse over the back of my chair, when Neil Samuelson slid into the seat across from me.

"No coffee?"

He glanced at the line. "I'll wait. What did you learn?"

One of CeCe's servers quietly set a warmed-up Danish by my elbow. I stopped to pull the plate in front of me. "Want some?"

"Yes." He reached for my plate.

I frowned at him. "I was just being polite."

"Then you probably shouldn't have offered it."

He had a point. He pulled off a third of my pastry and plopped it on a napkin in front of himself, taking time to lick frosting off his fingers.

He pushed the remaining pastry back in front of me, where I stared at it with my lips pursed. I really didn't like it when people took my food.

Samuelson wiped his mouth as the server set my chai latte on the table. He eyed my cup, so I grabbed it and took a quick drink from it. "Don't even think about it," I told him over narrowed eyes.

He smiled and picked up the pastry he had stolen from me. "Nah, I'm good. What did Allison Harris tell you?"

I related our conversation to Neil, who quickly pulled out his notebook and jotted in it while I talked.

"So she lied to me."

"Well, yes, but she had a good reason."

He looked up at me. "Everyone thinks they have a good reason." He flipped the notebook closed and tucked it back into his pocket. "But in my business, what it usually means is that they have something to hide, and it's never a good thing that they're hiding."

"She-" I stopped when he cocked a skeptical eyebrow at me. "I get that, detective, I do. She seemed like a scared kid to me."

I decided to change tactics. "What about Stormy McMaster? Allison said she applied for a job with her mom, but Patricia wouldn't hire her. Stormy sure didn't tell me about that when I talked to her."

Neil paused and rested his chin on a hand, staring at me pointedly. "And when exactly did you talk with Miss McMaster?"

Oops. I quickly lifted my mug and sipped the chai tea, scanning the area behind his shoulder for reinforcements. CeCe rang someone up at the register, chatting merrily with the customer, unaware that I was about to come under fire. I finally looked back at the detective.

"I might have visited her in the hospital."

"Your sister didn't mention that."

"She didn't know. I just visited Stormy because she was a yoga student and I wanted to make sure she was all right."

"Uh huh."

"Stormy might be worth taking a look at. Her history with Patricia isn't friendly. But I don't think Allison is our suspect. She just didn't strike me as a killer, that's all."

Neil grabbed the last bit of his – make that, *my* – pastry and stood up. "They never do, Ms. Stevens. They never do."

I couldn't help but mimic him. "*They never do, Ms. Stevens, they never do.*" I wasn't sure he heard me until his chuckle caught my ear. I rolled my eyes. I couldn't even insult the guy properly.

I sat back in my chair and sipped my chai tea, glancing over to see if the line had shortened and just in time to see CeCe and Paul talking, their heads together at the coffee bar. Then CeCe gently laughed and touched Paul's arm. When he smiled deep into her eyes, my mouth fell open. I sat up straighter and stared.

CeCe and Paul? How long had this been going on? I jumped out of my seat and scurried – yes, scurried is the only word for it – to CeCe. I grabbed a piece of skin behind her elbow and twisted, pulling her with me.

"Ouch!"

"Come with me," I hissed in her ear. "You have some explaining to do."

Just as we reached my table, she jerked away from me. "I think you left a bruise. What is the matter with you?"

I jerked a finger at the chair next to me. "Sit."

She sat.

I leaned toward her. "Paul?"

At first, CeCe looked confused. Then a small smile played at her mouth. "What about Paul?"

"Don't play innocent with me. Are you dating your barista?"

She looked past me and smiled again, this time I'm pretty sure it was at Paul. "I don't know that dating is the exact word you're looking for, but we've been ... seeing ... each other."

"You're his *boss*."

She shrugged. "He's been the manager here for a few years, but this is the first time we've both been single at the same time. What can I say, we hooked up."

"He's got to be ten years younger than you."

"Twelve." Her eyes danced.

"He's twelve years younger than you? That means he's still in his twenties." I couldn't tell if my face showed how horrified I felt about that, but apparently it didn't bother CeCe because she just laughed.

She reached over and laid a hand on my arm. "Look, it's not serious. We've always gotten along well and we're just having some fun."

I sat back and crossed my arms over my chest. "If you're sure. I just don't want you to get hurt again. It hasn't been that long since Jack left."

If ever a man were run out of town, it was CeCe's ex-husband, Jack. She not only took out an ad in the local newspaper telling the world about his multitude of affairs, but she also put a sign up in the café.

For the first time since he left, CeCe's face did not fall at the mention of her ex-husband. She shrugged again. "Just let me be happy for a while, okay?" I nodded slowly. "Besides, you've got Detective Hottie on your case, so you won't be lonely."

"I'm not lonely," I snapped, though truth be told there were times I actually was. I did miss having a man in my life. "Plus he works for my sister. And he thinks I might have killed someone."

CeCe stood up to return to the coffee bar. "I wouldn't write him off just yet, my friend." She laughed and danced away as I tried to swat her.

I checked my watch, surprised to see how much time had slipped away. Time for me to head back to the studio to prepare for the noon vinyasa class. I stood up to leave when someone grabbed my arm and jerked me into the booth just behind where I was sitting.

Chapter 13

"Hey! What you doing?" I looked at my attacker as I freed my arm. "Stormy?" As I rubbed my arm, I looked at her. "Why did you do that?"

She jabbed her thumb over the top of the booth. "You must not have seen me sitting here when you threw me under the bus to the detective."

My mouth fell open again, this time for a completely different reason, and I blushed. "You heard me—"

"Oh, yeah. I heard you say how I might have killed Patricia McMillan." Stormy's face turned red as her eyes squinted to slits. She jabbed me in the chest with her pointer finger, accentuating her words. "You better tell that detective I didn't do it because I didn't."

I pulled away from her and crossed my arms to protect my chest. "You were nearby when she died. You were mad at her because she wouldn't hire you and she treated you badly. You knew where she lived so you could have poisoned her at home."

Stormy's face grew darker. "So I just showed up at her door and said 'hey let me put something in your water bottle, Patricia? Have some tasty poison?'"

I sighed. It sounded worse when she put it like that. "Maybe I don't know how you did it, but I know I didn't do it, so it's got to be somebody else."

Stormy sat back in her seat, watching me. "Maybe you did do it and you're just trying to throw the blame on someone else, someone like me."

I pushed myself up out of the booth and turned to look at Stormy. "This conversation is over. If you have something to tell the sheriff's office, I suggest you do it, because I will be keeping my eyes on you."

I turned toward the door, waving to CeCe. I felt Stormy's eyes on me as I walked away. The nerve of that girl first eavesdropping on me and then accusing me of murder. I walked faster down the block, my hands shoved in my jacket pocket. The closer I got to the studio, the slower my steps became. If I hadn't been talking about her, she wouldn't have eavesdropped, and if I hadn't accused her first, she likely wouldn't have accused me either.

"Arrgh!" I yelled in frustration as I passed a young mom with a stroller, who jumped and hurriedly tried to move out of my way. I started to reach out toward her to appease her, but she rushed away.

I stopped when I got to the studio, resting my head on the door just before I opened it and took a deep breath. I didn't want to bring frustration with me into the studio. I stepped away from the door. Inhaling my hands over my head and down near my heart a few times, I brought myself back if not all the way to center, at least close enough that I wouldn't drag negative energy with me like a ball and chain into the studio. Then I reached up and brushed off my shoulders and neck as if wiping off lint. Instead, I felt as if I was wiping off negative energy that might have clamped down on me in the morning.

Satisfied, I finished unlocking the doors and stepped inside. I shrugged out of my jacket and walked into the studio, turning on lights as I went and plugging in the diffuser with an uplifting scent for the noon vinyasa class.

Vinyasa was my favorite class to teach, though it could be tricky to sequence. Each pose flowed into the next, heating up the body in the process. If I wasn't careful, I would have students standing when I wanted them on their mats or vice versa. I could always throw in a Downward Facing Dog pose to move students to the proper position, but I preferred to be more prepared than that. So I made sure to plan each class with the appropriate transitional poses.

As I set my mat down at the front of the class and toyed with which prop to use, noise erupted outside. I peeked through the curtains over the door to see Todd McMillan back in front of The Yoga Mat, waving his sign toward anyone who looked as if they were turning into the studio. He needn't have worried. Class didn't start for twenty-five minutes.

I dug in my purse for my cell, turning from the front door to block out the music from his boombox as I called for backups.

Five minutes later, Josie walked down the street from the other direction, meeting me at the studio door. She waved hello, then paused to take in the situation.

"Todd!" She called to him and waved him over. "C'mon over here, dude."

"I'm not your dude." He walked reluctantly toward her.

"You're acting like a dude." She looked at him in disgust, then spoke to him as if to a defiant child. "What did the judge say to you about this kind of activity?"

He stuck out his bottom lip and shrugged.

"Oh no, you don't," Josie warned. "You know exactly what the judge said. She said you have to stay fifty feet away from The Yoga Mat and that you cannot harass the owner, students, or anyone else connected with The Yoga Mat." She fixed him with a look. "Does that sound about right?"

McMillan looked up and away. Then he sighed and nodded.

"Then, sir, I will have to ask you to take your sign and your boombox and move along."

He stopped for a second, then pointed across the street. "Can I protest from over there?"

Josie looked across the street, then at McMillan, then at me. "Yes, you can," she admitted.

He picked up his sign and stomped across the street. "Don't make me arrest you for jaywalking," Josie muttered under her breath.

I stood at the little window in my office to watch McMillan. He stretched his arms wide and yawned, then shrugged his shoulders. Probably hadn't slept much since his wife died. Wait a minute, I told myself. Don't get all sympathetic toward this guy. He probably killed his wife, and if he did, then he didn't deserve a moment's rest.

While some of my noontime students came for relaxation, most of them came to work their muscles and rejuvenate themselves for the afternoon. I set my mat out, along with a block we would use, then sat down to ground myself in the few minutes before students began to show up for class.

This was my favorite time of the day. Quiet, reflective, peaceful. Then I heard the distant rumbling voice of Todd McMillan. I tried to bring my mind back to my mat; this usually works for me, but today, it was difficult to stay focused, so I stood and began a series of warmups, opting for a few rounds of Sun Salutations.

As I went through the poses, by habit I gave the cues in my head. "Inhaling as we raise our arms, reaching high over our heads, exhaling as we part our hands and hinge forward at the waist into a forward fold."

After a few moments, I caught myself smiling. Once again, the breath had brought me back to my place on the mat, to my place in the world. As my mentor teachers had told me and I often reminded my own students, our time on the mat was important. Everything else could be put aside for now.

The voice across the street got louder, apparently yelling at someone else. I hesitated, trying to stay grounded on my mat, but curiosity got the better of me and I hurried to the side of the front double doors and peeked out. The owner of the shop across the street was nose to nose with Todd McMillan, gesturing wildly for him to move away. Todd just kept pointing to my studio and would not back down.

The door swung out, startling me. Two of my noontime regulars stepped in and I ushered them into the lobby before they noticed McMillan. One of the two needed to pay for a new monthly pass and I was only too happy to stop my spying to take her money. That set off the before-class process, with students coming in, happily greeting each other and chatting.

For the rest of the day, it seemed that my door just kept popping open from students to the mail man to the landlord who wanted to check that a leak next door wasn't leaking into my bathroom. Then it was time to teach again. By the time I got home, I nibbled on a microwaved meal and fell into bed. It would be a while before I could sit and mull over what we had learned today.

The next morning, I awoke with questions about Patricia rolling around in my head. I knew one person could answer them, but first, I had a full morning of classes at The Yoga Mat. Just before the noontime class, a familiar voice checked in.

"Hey, sis."

Cindy stuck her head into my office. CeCe waved over Cindy's head and headed to her favorite corner in the back. My heart felt full as I glanced up to say hello. The greeting stuck in my throat as I saw Detective Neil Samuelson smiling just over Cindy's shoulder. Being in business mode, I tried to shove the smile back in place.

"I have a guest," Cindy smiled, her eyes laughing at me. "He would like to pay the drop-in fee."

Forget it. I let my smile fall and turned to Neil. "What are you doing here?"

"Yoga, I hope."

"No, seriously. Are you investigating me? Is that why you're here?" I whispered at him, trying not to make a scene in front of my students.

He shrugged. "One, I like yoga. Two, it can't hurt to get a feel for the place. Someone did die here, remember? Three, my boss invited me to come."

He smiled again. "And four, I like to support local businesses."

I turned to Cindy, who was already putting a waiver on a clipboard for Neil to fill out. If I could have shot darts with my eyes, I would have. "You invited him?"

I didn't wait for her response, just nodded at them both and scooted past them into the lobby to greet students. The door swung out and Melinda Jacobs walked in.

My eyes widened as she came directly to me and hugged me. "I'm so sorry about all the trouble Todd is causing you. Truly, he doesn't have the good sense of a mule."

"Thank you, Melinda. I'm so happy to see you in class."

She gently patted my arm. "Seeing you yesterday reminded me how much I missed my yoga."

I thanked her, then turned to greet another student.

Neil set up his mat in the back corner of the room. That's where most people who don't want to be noticed put their mats, typically people who either don't want anyone to see them or those who want to fly under the radar. *Interesting choice, detective.*

Cindy had picked her usual spot near the lobby door, where she could jump up to help if latecomers came in. Melinda was seated near the middle, chatting animatedly with another studio regular.

Just before class was set to start, the door opened again. Stormy McMaster barreled through. "I made it!"

Stormy slipped off her shoes while pulling her wallet out of her purse. She handed me a credit card. "I'd like a month pass, please." Her smile was triumphant. "If you're going to be keeping an eye on me, I'm going to keep mine on you. I figure the best way to do that is to be right here. With you. Every class I can." She smiled again.

I looked at her and sighed, then handed the card back to her. "You don't have to do that. Come for free."

She tried to hand the card back to me, but I picked up the sign-in sheet clipboard to match names to students before stopping to look at her. "I'm sure the doctor told you not to over-do it for a while. I'll help you modify where it's appropriate." Then I turned back to my class. Cindy leaned back to say something to Neil behind her. He laughed and shook his head, then paused to adjust his mat.

Stormy set up her mat in one of the few empty places on the floor, nearly in front of me.

At 18 students, the class was a good size. I brought everyone to a seated position and began centering them – and me. Our *pranayama*, the breathing technique, for this class was the complete yoga breath. It never failed to open my lungs and, metaphorically, my heart, bringing me into my practice.

I tried not to pay much attention to Stormy or to Neil, although it was hard. He did look good in a well-fit T-shirt and pair of light sweat pants. He was clearly strong and easily followed my cues. About two-thirds of the way through class, when most of my other students had at least broken a slight sweat, he looked sweat-free.

As our peak pose for the class, I brought everyone into Warrior 3, where students balanced on one leg as they bent at the waist and reached their hands out in front of them. Some placed a rectangular yoga block at the top of their mat to hang on to. A few, including Cindy and Neil, were able to stand without using the block.

As I gave instructions for students to adjust their poses and hold it for balance and strength, I noticed the detective fall out of his pose, catching himself before he went to the ground. He smiled and shrugged at no one in particular, then lifted himself back into the pose.

I gave the cue to do Warrior 3 on the other leg, reminding students that each side of our bodies are different, so it might feel harder or easier on this side. Neil had a little more trouble maintaining his balance on this side, but he quietly kept bringing himself back into the pose.

I don't know why that impressed me. *Yes, I do.* People who have a quiet perseverance keep improving themselves and moving forward. They are the best kind of yoga students.

Stormy struggled with Warrior 3, clearly still weak from her hospital stay. I quietly took her into a Half Forward Fold so she could begin strengthening core muscles without worrying about falling over. Sweat trickled down her face.

At the end of class, students put away the blankets and blocks they had used, talking companionably as they crowded the small lobby and gathered their mats and gear.

Cindy and Neil stayed behind talking as the other students rolled up their mats. I walked over to them while students were gathering their belongings in the lobby area by the cubbies.

"Good class, sis."

"Yeah, great class, Mariah. I feel energized." Neil's smile was warm and natural.

"Good. Now g-" I stopped myself before I said the words in my head ("Now go catch the real killer."). "Go have a peaceful day, and thank you for helping to solve Patricia's murder."

Cindy wrapped me in a hug. I hugged her in return, then stepped back and whispered to her, "Now, get that murder solved."

Chapter 14

Only a few students remained after class. Melinda sat on a chair in the corner pulling on her boots and fidgeting with her phone. Stormy stood next to the sign-in table, an expectant look on her face.

"Yes, Stormy. Can I help you?" I said it, but I didn't really mean it.

"What do we do now?"

"Excuse me?"

"What's our next step to find out who killed Patricia? Hey!" I grabbed Stormy by the arm and dragged her into my office. I know, I *know*, not exactly yoga-teacher-friendly. "Why did you do that?"

I put my index finger to my lips in the *shhh* motion. When she stopped talking, I pointed toward the lobby and whispered to Stormy. "That's Patricia's sister, Melinda. Please don't upset her further by discussing how Patricia died."

Stormy peeked out the door at Melinda, then ducked back in. "Okay, but that's what you've been doing, right?" she whispered. "Looking for the killer? Well, you're not doing it without me."

I stared at Stormy, grinding my teeth together. "No, you cannot come with me."

"I can help," she whispered back.

"No, Stormy, it's too dangerous."

She put her mouth next to my ear. "Then I will follow you every where you go. You are not getting rid of me that easily."

"Bye, Mariah." Melinda called as she pulled her purse from the cubbies on the other side of the lobby. We waved to each other and she set off out the door.

"Stormy, you have to go now. I have a client coming in shortly. It's a private session, so you can't be here."

Stormy stood in the lobby, looking around as if she planned to duck under a chair, then reached for her sandals and pulled them on. As she pushed open the door, she looked back. "I'm watching you, Mariah Stevens."

As the door was closing, I couldn't help but mimic her. "I'm watching you, Mariah Stevens. Ugh."

The door popped back open.

"I heard that." Stormy then pulled the door shut with a bang.

I tiptoed to the door and peeked out to see if she was really gone. As I went to look the opposite way, I pushed the door into my client. She jumped back with an exclamation.

"I am so sorry." I gently took her arm and led her into the studio. This day had not gone anything like I expected it to, but at least

Stormy seemed to be gone for now. I turned my attention back to my work.

After my private session, I tucked my purse over my shoulder, locked the front doors of the studio and stepped out the back. I had barely clicked the locks on my car doors open when Stormy McMaster appeared at the passenger side, flung open the door and hopped inside.

"What are you doing?" My voice was severely higher than usual.

"I'm going with you."

"You don't know where I'm going."

"Where are you going?"

Too startled to think clearly, I stammered out, "the-the-the grocery store."

"No, you're not. You eat at the diner all the time. You wouldn't leave your studio in the middle of the day to go grocery shopping. I don't think you even buy groceries."

I sat up straight in the driver's seat and stared at her. "I do so buy groceries."

She tilted her head and looked at me pointedly.

"Not that often," I conceded.

"So where are you going?"

"To see Allison Harris. I have some questions about her mother."

"I'm going with you."

"No, you're not."

"Yes, I am."

"You're. Not. Going." I didn't see how I could be any more forceful without physically shoving her out of the car.

Stormy leaned back against the passenger window. "I know Allison from middle school. I can help you. And it will be easier for you to take me with you than for you to try to get me out of this car."

She turned in the seat and pulled down on the seat belt, clicking it into place, then folding her arms and looking at me.

Sighing, I started the car and pulled out of the alley toward Patricia's house.

We drove in silence, thank goodness. About halfway there, I realized Stormy was watching me.

I flicked my eyes toward here. "What?"

"Nothing. You just don't look like what I expected yoga teachers to look like, that's all, and you don't act like one, either."

I sighed. "Gee, thanks for that."

I kept my eyes on the road. "Actually, I hear that a lot. I'm not a rubber band and I have a few extra pounds. I know I don't look like your typical yoga instructor." I took my eyes off the road and looked at her, our eyes meeting. "But that's not what yoga is about, Stormy."

"Yoga is about matching movement to breath and letting yourself be breathed by life. It's about trying to do the next right thing and being content with yourself both on and off the mat. That's what attracted me to yoga in the first place. By the way, I used to weigh a lot more before I started doing yoga."

"Really?" Stormy looked surprised. "I thought you had to do cardio to lose weight."

"Sometimes. But sometimes you have to get comfortable enough with yourself that you make better nutrition choices."

I glanced at her out of the corner of my eye as I made the left turn past the Old Gym. "I appreciate you being honest with me. Now I have a question for you."

"O-kay." She sounded uncertain.

"Do you like your body? Have you ever tried to lose weight or change your body?"

Stormy fell silent, looking away from me out the passenger window. "I, um, I used to be anorexic."

I nodded to myself. Everybody – even beautiful twenty-somethings – have something.

"What happened?"

"I never felt like I fit in and never felt good about myself. I wasn't one of the smart kids or the talented kids. We didn't have much money, so I wasn't one of the rich kids." She barked out a quick laugh. "I couldn't afford to do drugs, so I wasn't even one of the stoners." She laughed again, a more natural laugh this time. "The only thing I could do was control how I looked. I was terrified of gaining weight, so mostly I just didn't eat. It wasn't like I was going to eat food and throw it up. That's way too wasteful."

Pulling through an intersection, I threw a glance her way. "We're not that different, you and me. I'm just a couple decades older, so I've figured a few things out."

We stopped the car in front of Patricia's house. Todd was still protesting across the street from the studio, or maybe he had gone into the bar by now, so we wouldn't run into him this time.

We rang the bell. Allison opened it, looking considerably better than she had the last time I saw her. A smile broke across her face.

"Stormy!" Allison pulled her in for a hug, then stood back and looked at her. "It's been too long. You look great."

Stormy blushed and returned the compliment, then Allison ushered us into the house and into the living room where we had sat before.

"What are you doing here?"

Stormy pointed to me. "I'm helping Mariah look into your mom's death, and we had a few more questions."

Allison shrugged. "Okay. Like what?"

Stormy looked at me as if passing the floor to me, so I jumped in.

"So, did your friend agree to be your alibi?"

Allison shot Stormy a look when I asked the question. Then she carefully nodded. "She said of course, if it helps me."

Stormy squeezed Allison's hand. "It's okay, Ally. We all knew in high school, even if you didn't."

Allison pulled her hand away and sat up straight. "What you mean you *knew*?"

"That you're gay. It's okay. Didn't you wonder why we kept finding you new 'friends' to hang with?"

Allison stared at Stormy, then started to laugh. "You were trying to hook me up?"

Stormy nodded, then joined in the laughter. The two women hugged, then sat back in comfortable silence.

"I don't know if the sheriff's office told you, but your mom left my studio some money in her will. I was surprised. What can you tell us about your mom? What did she do for a living that she had so much money to throw around?"

Allison nodded. "The deputy told us. The money she left you was a very small part of what she had. She worked in IT, actually Mom and Aunt Melinda both worked in IT for a long time." She looked down at her hands and her eyes flicked to Stormy, who took one of her hands in her own. Allison smiled at her. "The bulk of Mom's money, however, came from all of her divorces. She never married well, but she divorced *extremely* well."

"She must have been a very bright woman to be in IT."

Allison smiled more broadly, her eyes sad. "Super smart. She and Aunt Mel both. But it wasn't just esoteric smart or just smart like writing codes and things. I mean, Aunt Mel even installed our security system."

"You're kidding?" That sounded like something I'd definitely hire someone to do for me.

"Yeah, it only took her a few hours one afternoon and she had it done. She wouldn't even let Mom pay for it. It really helped Mom feel safer, you know, whenever Todd was out late at the bars or wherever."

"That sounds like an expensive gift."

"I guess, but Aunt Mel seemed to be doing better in the past couple of years. I guess she must have saved a lot because all of a sudden, she was spending quite a bit."

I could relate. "I know how great it is to have a sister I can depend on. Family is so important."

"I don't know about that," Allison laughed. "Mom and Aunt Mel seemed to argue more and more in the past year."

"Do you know what they argued about?"

She shook her head. "I think it had to do with work, but I couldn't say for sure. Todd might be able to tell you more."

Stormy and I exchanged an eye-roll over Allison's head. I was pretty sure I wouldn't get any information from Todd McMillan.

"No offense, Ally, but Todd doesn't sound like much of a prize." Stormy jumped into the conversation.

Allison shrugged and leaned back against the sofa. "He can be really sweet when he's not drinking. He's not what you would call sophisticated, but he's not a bad guy."

Inwardly, I scoffed. Maybe not so inwardly because Stormy raised her eyebrows at me, then turned her attention back to Allison.

"Ally, did Todd know your mom was thinking of divorcing him?"

Allison nodded again and gripped Stormy's hands. "He knew. In fact, he wondered why it took so long. I think that's why he started drinking more. Kind of made it a self-fulfilling prophecy, you know?"

I smiled at them both, then I gave Stormy a head nod that it was time to leave. Within a few minutes, we were back in my car and driving back into town. I dropped Stormy at her apartment, promising I would call her if I got another lead. Stormy actually had helped during my talk with Allison, and, although I hated to admit it, she was starting to grow on me.

Chapter 15

My next two classes of the day went smoothly. At least, no one died. I was starting to count that as a "win" in my classes. The second class was a Restorative Yoga class, which left students and me a little drowsy.

After the last student left, I let my body expand into one long stretch, wiggling my arms and fingers over my head. I set about to tidy up before Tabitha came in to teach the last class of the night when my cell phone *dinged*. Broom in one hand, I swiped to see a message: *Got a lead on Patricia's killer. Meet me at the Old Gym at 10:00 tonight. – Stormy.*

That sounded promising. I wondered why she wanted to meet at the Old Gym, then remembered her apartment was near there and shrugged. I hung out at the studio until Tabitha showed for the last class. I reminded her to announce the upcoming workshops, then headed out the door. Glancing at the time on my cell, I had plenty of time to make it to the gym by ten o'clock.

The parking lot was empty when I pulled up, which didn't surprise me. I suspected Stormy walked from her apartment complex. As I got out of my car, I half-expected her tall, lanky frame to pop out of the shadows, but I didn't see anything. Maybe I had beat her here. I lifted my head above the car.

"Stormy? Stormy, are you here?"

The faint sound of metal on metal sounded near the front of the school, so I pulled out my phone to use as a flashlight and trekked across the parking lot. There was too much concrete waste to park very close to the building. I pulled on the heavy metal door and peeked inside.

"Mariah? Is that you?" A faint voice called from inside.

Throwing open the door with all my strength, I paused to listen. "Stormy? Is that you?"

"Yes, I fell into the floor. Why did you yell for me to come this way?"

I gingerly stepped into the gymnasium. Wooden bleachers lay cracked and broken, sharp pieces dangling as if they'd been sheared away. The floor itself was littered with holes and craters. In the darkness, I could see the top of Stormy's head across the gym.

"What did you say?"

"I asked you why you yelled at me to come this way across the gym. Obviously, it's dangerous. I could have broken my neck."

I looked around me. "Stormy, I just got here. I didn't yell at you to do anything. I didn't even know you would be here."

"What? Of course it was you. Who else would yell at me?"

A *ping* sounded off to my left. I yelped and leapt to the right, losing my footing and falling to the floor. Another *ping* sounded nearby, then another.

"Stormy, get down!" I screamed. "Someone is shooting at us!" As bullets rained toward us, I crawled as fast as I could toward bleachers near Stormy. One grazed my arm and I screamed again, jamming that arm into the side of a hole in the floor, my knee plunging through and my body tumbling into the darkness.

"Mariah!" Stormy's hushed voice carried across the now silent gym. "Mariah, are you okay?"

I spit dirt out of my mouth, then jumped as I felt something crawl across my right hand. "Arggh!" Then I bumped my head on the floor above me. Reaching back to rub the sore spot, I realized that I had only fallen a few feet through the subfloor. Thank goodness the Old Gym didn't have a basement or I would have more severe injuries.

Turning back toward the hole I had fallen through, I reached out and pulled myself up. Pieces of floor kept breaking off in my hands, slowing my progress.

"Stormy, I think I'm all right." I finally crawled out and dug my cell phone out of my back pocket. No service in this concrete building, but at least I could use the flashlight app. Coming up to my feet, I pointed it in the general direction of Stormy. "Say something so I can find you."

"Mariah, this is crazy. I can't believe someone shot at us and tried to kill us. I just kept hearing the bullets and then you fell in the floor and then everything went quiet."

"Did you hear anyone else here?" I walked carefully toward Stormy, checking my weight on the floor before stepping further.

Stormy was silent for a moment. "I heard feet running and a door shut, then nothing. Do you see me?"

"Almost there." I reached the crater Stormy had fallen into and knelt down beside her. "Are you hurt?"

"My ankle and my shoulder. "

"Use your good side and I'll help pull your other side." I reached down toward Stormy and braced myself, hoping the floor would hold both of our weight. "On three, let's get you out."

I gently pulled from around Stormy's waist as Stormy pressed into the floor to lift herself up. Within a few seconds, she was lying face down on the floor, gasping for breath.

"We'll have to crawl out," I told Stormy. "It's just too unstable."

We crawled gingerly toward the exit, Stormy wobbling on three limbs and me feeling burning in my arm from where the bullet apparently had scraped my arm.

Agonizingly slow, we made progress. When we reached the door, we leaned against each other to stand, then tottered together through the door and into the fresh night air.

Stormy began to sob as I put an arm around her and led her to my car.

"I thought I was going to die in there, Mariah." She sniffled and gasped.

I kept an arm around her, rubbing her back and trying to comfort her. "How did you get here Stormy and why did you want me to meet you here?"

Stormy leaned against the hood of my car, looking at me in surprise. "I walked. I just live around the corner in those brown apartments. What do you mean, why did I want to meet you here?"

"I got a text saying you had information about Patricia's killer and that you had to show it to me at the Old Gym."

Stormy stared at me. "I got the same text. Only it said *you* had the information, so I walked over here to meet you."

We stared at the ground, then I suddenly looked up. Whoever had been here was long gone. Why had we been lured out to the Old Gym?

"We're getting close to Patricia's killer." Stormy lifted her chin and looked at me. "They're trying to get rid of us."

"That can't be right." I dropped my chin to my chest. "We literally have no idea who killed her."

"You know that and I know that, but the killer doesn't know that."

"Okay, I'll call Cindy when I get back to town and let her know what happened. Let me get you home."

Stormy stood up as straight as her ankle would let her, eyes wide. "No way. My roommate is out of town and I'm not going home to an empty apartment. Someone tried to kill me tonight."

I looked at Stormy warily. Was she telling the truth? I couldn't be sure. I was beginning to wonder who I could trust.

"Please, Mariah. Can I come home with you?"

Stormy's face was pleading. I decided to give her the benefit of the doubt. I nodded slowly. "Okay. Let's go to my house. If there is a killer out here, I don't want to be alone either."

If I'm taking one home with me, I thought, well, that's a completely different problem.

Chapter 16

After letting Stormy have first dibs on the downstairs bath, then bandaging her injuries, which didn't seem all that serious, I heated up soup for both of us and settled Stormy on the couch in the den.

She seemed snug and warm and already falling asleep when I said good night and softly closed the door, leaving the desk lamp on because Stormy felt freaked out by the dark.

Sinking into the tub upstairs, I let the hot water engulf me, even dunking my head for a moment. Settling into the bubbles, I closed my eyes and let my mind run back over the events of the past few days.

Was Todd McMillan the one who shot at Stormy and me? Why did he seem to have it in for me? His assessment of me and The Yoga Mat seemed way out of bounds. Patricia and I hadn't socialized. I didn't even know her outside of the studio. McMillan seemed awfully fixated on me as the killer. Perhaps he really was just trying to deflect from himself.

I leaned my neck back, rolling it gently from side to side as I let that idea roll around. He didn't seem to have it in him to be that deceptive, but looks can be deceiving and I, of all people, knew better than to judge the proverbial book.

My eyes flew open as my phone buzzed on the bathroom counter. I closed them again, knowing whoever it was would leave a message or call back. So they did. The phone buzzed repeatedly as if someone was just redialing and redialing.

I pulled myself out of the tub, wrapping a towel around me and reached for the phone as it buzzed again. I pressed the button before seeing who had called. "Hello?"

"Mariah, it's Tabitha." Her voice shook. "Someone threw a rock through the studio window. You need to get down here right now."

I gasped. "Are you okay? Are you hurt?"

"No, I mean, yes, I'm okay. Just hurry."

I threw down the phone and dried off in record time, pulling back on the clothes I had just tossed on the floor.

I was nearly to the studio when I remembered Stormy asleep in my house. I pressed on. When I screeched to a halt in front of the studio, Neil Samuelson in a T-shirt and jeans – clearly he had been called from home – and a sheriff's deputy stood outside, talking and gesturing, turning as I sprinted toward them. I stopped at the center of the glass window, staring at the gash and a thousand little cracks. Anger rushed through my body as I turned toward the detective.

"What in the hell is going on? Why is someone attacking my studio?" My arms flung around in large movements of their own accord, prompting the two law enforcement officers to back away.

"Mariah, calm down." Even as he said the words, Neil looked like he didn't believe I would. Does anyone calm down when you tell them to? *No, the answer is no.*

"I will not calm down." My voice was louder and higher than I would've liked, but I hardly cared. "Someone is trying to put me out of business. Who is doing this? Why can't you find out and stop them?"

I clutched my arms around myself at the elbows and stared at Neil. Mournful eyes looked back at me. He gently put his arms around me. I started to stiffen up, then exhaled and laid my head on his shoulder, tears streaming down my face and onto his shirt.

The detective patted my back, letting his chin rest on my head.

I sobbed into his shirt, then eased back, wiping my face with the ends of my sleeves wrapped around my hands for comfort. "Thank you."

Embarrassed for my tears, my eyes couldn't quite meet his, so I turned toward the studio door. Deputies already were hammering boards over the window.

"What exactly happened?"

Tabitha bolted through the door and flung herself into my arms. "Mariah, thank goodness!"

Through tears and gulps, my young yoga instructor told me what had happened. She had closed the studio earlier but had forgotten her cell phone. She parked in the alley and slipped in through the back when she heard a loud crash from the lobby window.

"I think I screamed," she gulped.

I patted her back. "I would've, too."

She heard steps like someone running off, then the squealing sound of a car peeling away. I turned to look at the window, then back at Tabitha.

"The important thing is that no one was hurt. Can she go home?" My question was directed to Neil. He nodded.

"I think we have all we need from her right now."

Tabitha gave me another hug, then started around the back of the building to her car. I gestured to Neil to go with her, which he in turn got the deputy to do.

I stared at the front of my studio. "I wish now that I had put in those security cameras when the City Council was talking everyone into them."

Neil shrugged. "Don't worry about it. Someone around here has a video or saw something." He stepped back and eyeballed me. "We'll *know*."

I did a double-take and stared at him. "Oh, good grief. You think I threw a brick through my own studio window? Are you insane?"

The detective shrugged. "Mariah, I ha-"

I waved him off. "I know, I know. You have to cover all the angles. Got it." I started to turn away, then looked back. "And it's Ms. Stevens to you, Detective Samuelson."

"OK, *Ms. Stevens*, can you account for your whereabouts the past few hours?"

I jolted and looked at him. How was I going to explain what had happened to Stormy and me? "Why? Do you think I was searching the junkyard for a brick to throw into my own studio?"

"Where were you?" He spoke so quietly I barely heard him.

"If you must know, someone lured me to the Old Gym and shot at me until I fell through the flooring."

Neil's eyes nearly popped out of his head. "Are you okay? Why didn't you report it?"

I held up my arm, which Stormy had helped me bandage to answer his first question. "I was too busy taking care of Stormy McMaster, who also got lured there and suffered injuries."

"But you didn't think to report it, even though your sister is the sheriff?"

My mouth opened a few times, but no words came out. My shoulders dropped.

"I meant to. I was just so exhausted," I whispered. "I couldn't deal with it anymore."

His eyes appraised me, then he nodded. "Okay. We'll need to go out to the Old Gym tomorrow to look around and corroborate your story."

He dipped his head as the officer who was sweeping up came outside, brushing off his hands. "All done. You can go inside now."

I shook my head. I just wasn't ready to face any more drama tonight. Locking the front door, I gave a tug on the door handle, then turned back to my car.

"Good night, Ms. Stevens."

I waved a hand behind me. That would have to do.

Chapter 17

The next morning, I sat at my kitchen table, its vintage wood typically a source of cool comfort. Today, my hands gripped the mug.

"Not enough coffee in the world to get through today," I muttered to myself.

Defeat and failure oozed from my pores as I set my mug aside and put my head on the table. This was a first for me. Not once in the nearly nine months since I had opened The Yoga Mat had I not wanted to go to work. The studio was my sanctuary. I loved doing yoga and helping others to do it, too. What would I say to a client in this position?

I took a breath, filling my chest and exhaled slowly. Then again. My head began to clear. I would tell my client that we can't always dictate what happens to us, but we *can* dictate how we respond.

I looked at the mug in my hand, pulling back my arm as if I would hurl it into the wall. How would I respond? I took another breath and set the cup on the table. No, I told myself. Today, I choose to respond with hope. I closed my eyes and settled into the word. *Hope.*

Another deep breath, then I stood up and threw back my shoulders. *Okay, day, bring it on.*

"Mariah?" You up?" Stormy padded into the kitchen, walking gingerly on her left ankle.

Motioning for her to sit, I jumped up to get her a cup of coffee and set it down before her. I heated a blueberry muffin in the microwave and set it down with a napkin.

"How are you feeling?" I finally asked, searching her face for signs of what, I didn't even know. She had slept through the night on my couch. In fact, she hadn't even stirred when I slipped back through the front door after meeting the deputies at the studio. I know because I had peeked into the den on my way upstairs.

She shrugged, looking small and lost in the oversized t-shirt she had borrowed from me, with dark rings under her eyes that matched my own. "I've never had anyone actually try to kill me before," she said slowly, her eyes on her mug. "When I drank from Patricia's water bottle and got sick, that was just an accident for me. It was Patricia they were after."

I nodded, slumping down in my chair.

"What are we going to do about it?" Her words were defiant.

Ours eyes met and we both sighed, then weakly laughed. I told her about the detective wanting to meet us at the Old Gym. First, however, I needed to take her home and begin to make calls about fixing the studio window.

After dropping Stormy at her apartment, I felt the need to be out and about in the community. I wanted my neighbors to know I wasn't a killer. Stopping at the Corner Mercantile, I bought a basket, ribbon and filler.

Sandy Anderson, the owner, smiled from behind the cash register. "Getting your basket ready for the big event?"

I nodded and showed her what I had, then chatted about what I intended to fill it with.

Sandy oohed and ahhed. "I keep meaning to try one of your classes, Mariah, but I've been so busy with the store and all." She waved a hand around her shop, then put my items in a bag.

"Why don't you come in for a free class?" I reached into a pocket of my purse and took out a business card. On the back, I wrote "Good for one free class," then initialed it. I told Sandy to give it to any of the instructors and they would honor it, even if I wasn't there. From another pocket, I pulled out a class schedule. "There are a lot of options, Sandy, so come join us."

I sounded more cheerful than I felt, but I knew I had to make the effort. If this murder made business fall off, my fledgling studio was doomed.

The first classes of the day were small, as if my students felt my own lethargy. We took it easy, trying to raise the positive energy in the room.

Just after the noon class, I drove out to the Old Gym, stopping to pick up Stormy on the way. Her limp was less pronounced and she seemed stronger, wiggling her shoulder when I asked about it.

Neil showed up with a couple of patrolmen and a K-9 unit. They opened the doors and used blocks to hold them back to let in some light. Stormy and I eased carefully inside, staying near the door and pointing across the gym to where we each had been and where we thought the bullets had come from. The detective listened impassively, then let the dogs and their officers out on the floor. They crept right to where Stormy and I had fallen through the floor, whimpering when the flooring began to shift beneath them.

Stormy huddled beside me as Neil asked her the same questions he had asked me – where had the text come from, why had she gone inside and what happened after I got there.

"Could you see Mariah the whole time?"

Stormy nodded, then stopped and frowned. "Well, not really. I could see her outline a little bit, but it was super dark."

Neil wrote that down in his notebook. "Could you see where the bullets were coming from?"

Stormy shook her head violently, her young face darkening as she remembered. She waved her arms to demonstrate. "I could hear them hitting around me. They whooshed and then there would be a little thud."

I nodded. That's what I had experienced, too. He didn't ask me, however. He took Stormy's arm and walked her away from me, turning back to motion me to stay where I was. My mouth fell open as I realized what he thought.

"Wait a minute!" I rushed over to him and grabbed his arm, flinging him backward. The two deputies started in my direction, but Neil put out a hand to stop them.

"You think I lured Stormy out here and then shot at her? What kind of a person do you think I am?"

"You're the kind that will go to jail if you grab a deputy like that again." Neil's eyes were dark. I could tell that even in the shadows of the Old Gym. "Now stay over there until I'm done talking with Miss McMaster."

This could not be happening. I turned and stalked outside, stopping at my car and kicking the tire. A deputy parked herself outside to keep an eye on me. I threw myself into the front seat and dropped my head between my legs as I struggled to control my emotions.

I was in trouble. I picked up my cell phone to text the one person who might be able to help me.

Sis, your detective thinks I tried to kill Stormy. I think he's going to throw me in jail.

Silence.

Cindy?

Nothing. The knot in my stomach grew tighter as I waited. She was never far from her cell phone. Finally, her response came.

Trust the process. Not supposed to talk to you about the case.

I stared at the phone. *You're my sister.*

And the sheriff.

My breath caught in my throat. So that was how it was. I knew when I moved to Jasper that things might be different between us. We hadn't lived in the same town for more than twenty years. I just didn't think her job would come between us.

Trust the process, Cindy said. Or maybe I should peel out of the parking lot and go into hiding until this nightmare was over. I reached for my keys from where I'd tossed them on the passenger's seat.

"Ms. Stevens?"

I dropped my hand and looked up to meet Neil's eyes. "Can you show me the text that was sent to you?"

I pulled out my cell and quickly swiped to Messages, found the one from last night and handed him the phone. He took at picture of the screen. "That matches with what Miss McMaster showed us." He handed back the phone. "I'll have our tech folks see if they can run down where it originated from."

I rolled my eyes and tossed my phone on the seat by the keys. "Are we through here, detective?"

"Just one more thing, Ms. Stevens. That brick that was thrown through your studio window last night? Care to know where it came from?"

I stared at the detective, then let my gaze drift toward the Old Gym. "It didn't."

"It did. We'll return Miss McMaster to her apartment."

I nodded, reaching for the door handle of my car and slamming the door shut. Tears of anger and panic welled up and I let them fall down my face, not even bothering to try to wipe them off.

Workers were waiting for me at the studio to replace the window, so I brushed away my tears and forced myself to walk into my office. I put a citrus scent into the defuser, hoping to lift my own spirits before the noon class.

By the time noon rolled around, the energy in the studio felt better. The noon class had been large and a couple of students had brought new students with them to try out the studio. A wave of gratitude washed over me as the workers finished, tidying up after themselves and leaving the studio quiet for the first time in hours.

Opening my laptop in the office, I began to plan workshops for the coming months – anything to take my mind off the noose that Detective Samuelson seemed to be tightening around my neck.

I focused on the workshops. They gave students the opportunity to deepen their practice and also bring in extra revenue for the studio. I was toying with a pranayama class on breathing techniques or perhaps a more advanced class for my fitter students.

The front door swung open. Neil and a sheriff's deputy burst into the lobby. I jumped up and met them at the door. "What's going on?"

The deputy looked at Neil, who nodded. "Ma'am, we have a warrant to search the premises."

Neil jumped in. "Mariah, I mean, Ms. Stevens, we have reason to believe that you have something stored at the studio that might be relevant to the Patricia McMillan case."

"Again, why? You already searched the studio the night Patricia died."

Neil shook his head and launched into an explanation about how they only gave a cursory examination because there was no hard evidence to tie her death to the studio. "Until now."

He nodded to the deputy, who apparently had been coached beforehand, so he sat down in the lobby and carefully removed his shoes. Neil did the same, then followed the officer across the studio floor to the closet where mats, blocks, blankets and other gear are stored on shelves that students can reach. The bottom shelves are devoted to cleaning and other supplies for the studio.

I followed them to the closet, peering around them. "What are you looking for?"

"Aha!" The officer reached behind some antiseptic wipes and carefully dislodged a small brown bottle. Even I could see the big red "X" on it from outside the closet.

He eased the bottle into a bag that Neil held, then took the bag and headed back to the lobby for his shoes.

The detective looked at the ground, then looked at me. "Ms. Stevens, I'm placing you under arrest for the murder of Patricia McMillan."

Chapter 18

I sat at a small table in a dank room at the sheriff's post and sighed. Whoever was trying to put me out of business was doing a bang-up job at it. I had texted Tabitha and Cindy to see if they could juggle the rest of the day's classes before the deputy took my phone.

The door quietly opened and Samuelson stepped through. He set the baggie with the little brown bottle on the table then quickly pressed buttons on a machine that sat on the table and told me that we were being recorded.

He had trouble making eye contact. *Good.* I sat back, crossed my arms and stared coldly at him.

"Ms. Stevens, what can you tell me about this bottle?"

I stared at him. He waited.

"Nothing. I've never seen it before. Did you run it for prints, Mr. Detective? You'll find my prints aren't on it."

"How would you know that?"

"Because I've never seen it before."

Samuelson sat back and stared at me. "Ms. Stevens, I need you to cooperate."

My mouth fell open. "Cooperate? I have done nothing but cooperate and yet here I am. I'm done. Call my lawyer."

He pursed his lips and slammed the buttons on the machine, then snatched the plastic bag off the table and stomped out the door, slamming it behind him.

Moments later, the door opened and Josie stepped in. "Mariah, you need to come with me." Her voice was quiet but firm. She held the door open for me, then guided me down a hallway I had never been before until we reached a heavy metal door. Josie unlocked three locks on the door, then opened it, motioning me through.

I stopped and stared, then turned toward Josie. Inside the door were a half dozen holding cells. "He's locking me up? This is crazy. Josie, you know I didn't do this."

I pulled away as Josie took my arm, but she held me firmly, leading me to the nearest cell, opening the door and guiding me through. She closed the door behind me and paused.

"I'm sorry," she whispered as a tear slipped down her cheek. Without looking back at me, she turned toward the metal door and pulled it shut behind her.

I sat down hard on the metal bed, tears streaming down my face.

"You gotta be kiddin' me." I heard shuffling at the cell on the opposite side. I lifted my head to look and my heart sank. Todd McMillan.

"You've got to be kidding *me*," I whispered to myself as I turned away.

"They finally sthrew your ash in jail for killing my Patsy." He slurred his words. "Mel was right. She kept telling me it wush you. I love Mel. Shesh always got my back. Yep, yep."

I wouldn't turn around to look at him. He stumbled about and I heard a loud CLANG.

Wheeling around, I could see him lying half on the metal cot and half off. He didn't move. Gulping, I moved to the edge of my cell for a better look.

"Todd? Mr. McMillan? Are you all right?"

After a few moments, he gave a big open-mouthed yawn, then slumped to the floor, apparently passed out.

I clenched my fists and yelled silently at the ceiling. What was I doing here? They couldn't possibly think I had killed Patricia. Where was my sister and why wasn't she helping me?

When I wanted to smash the sides of the cell bars with my fists, I stopped and took a deep breath. Inhaling, I lifted my arms over my head. Exhaling, I parted my hands and swan-dived forward into a forward fold. Connecting to my breath, I breathed my way through a set of Sun Salutations, ignoring the state of the cement floor. I'd shower later. Right now, I needed to calm my mind and body. I continued with Sun Sal after Sun Sal, even through the snoring of my cellmate across the room.

After a couple of hours, my lawyer arrived. I held my head high as I walked beside him out of the Sheriff's post, not wanting to see the stares of my sister's coworkers.

We stopped at the studio so I could get my car, then I drove home. My phone rang. "Cindy." I ignored it. Then "Josie." I ignored her, too. They had let me sit in a jail cell. I turned off the phone and stuck it on the charger, then went upstairs to shower.

I stepped out of the steamy bathroom wrapped in a towel with another one around my wet hair, feeling somewhat refreshed but still angry and became aware of banging at my back door. I tiptoed downstairs and peeked through the kitchen doorway.

"Mariah! I know you're in there. Let me in!" Cindy banged again.

I walked to the kitchen door, stared at my sister through the glass and pulled down the shade. Then I turned and stomped back upstairs to change into my clothes.

When I came downstairs, the banging had moved to the front door. I stopped at the foot of the stairs, where I could see out through the glass. CeCe waved.

Hmm. Cindy had brought reinforcements. Much as I wanted to shut them all out, I also really wanted my friends around me. It was time to let them in, so I threw open the door.

CeCe shoved a cup in my hand. "Double caramel mocha with whip."

I accepted, then set it on the occasional table just inside the door. Turning back to CeCe, I flung myself into her arms. She hugged me fiercely. As other arms joined on top of hers, I tried to struggle out of the hug, but they held me tight. Finally, I relaxed and let them hug me. When I finally lifted my head, I looked into the faces of my two best friends and my sister.

"You can stay." I nodded at CeCe, then turned to the other two. "You can go. You left me in a jail cell for three hours."

Josie and Cindy looked at the floor, then back at me. "We know. There was nothing we could do. Neil is in charge of the case, sweetie." Cindy shook her head. "I tried to talk him out of it, but I could only push so much."

I glared at her. "Are you sure it's not because you're up for re-election soon?"

She sighed deeply and directed her eyes at mine. "It would make no difference, sis. I can't be seen as overstepping my authority. It would undermine the integrity of the sheriff's office."

"It would undermine the integrity of the sheriff's office." I mimicked her voice. "It was gross. Plus Todd McMillan was there."

Josie nodded. "We hauled him in for drunk and disorderly earlier today. He's a mess."

She closed the door behind them. "We do need to talk, though."

We scooted down the hall and into the kitchen. As we sat around my cheerful table, Josie leaned toward me. "Think, Mariah. Who could have put the arsenic in your studio closet? Who had access?"

I held out my arms akimbo. "I've been asking myself that question. It could have been anyone who came into the studio."

I tried to remember when I had last looked deep into the studio closet. Thinking out loud, I told them how I had bought extra wipes on sale Saturday and put them in their place on the bottom shelf. We were almost out and students who used the studio's mats cleaned them with the wipes after class. I had moved a few things around on the shelf to make room for the extras. I had also done the deep clean right after Patricia had died.

"I'm positive I would have noticed a bottle of poison with an 'X' on it." I looked around the table to faces as impassive as my own.

"The back door is always locked, even when we are there," Cindy added. "So no one could have come in that way, and the front doors are locked when an instructor isn't there."

Silence settled in around the table. Finally, I said what no one else wanted to say.

"They came through the front door." My voice was barely a whisper and even I could feel defeat oozing out of it.

"So you know whoever it is." Josie summed it up.

I shuddered. "Except I don't. Whoever did this has been wearing a mask, letting me believe they're someone they're not."

Josie cleared her throat. "Has there been anyone in class this week you didn't know or that was a surprise?"

I shrugged. A few new students had signed up for passes, but I had never met them and they had no reason to plant poison on me or kill Patricia, as far as I knew. I hated the idea that one of my students might hate me so much that she or he would set me up like that.

I lifted my head and looked Cindy in the eye. "Detective Samuelson. He was new. He could've brought the poison in just to set me up."

Cindy held my gaze. "Stop it. Neil did not bring arsenic with him. I was between him and the closet the whole time he was there."

She paused and looked at me. "But you know who was a surprise in that class?"

I thought back to the class. "Melinda?"

"I was thinking Stormy McMaster."

I shook my head at both suggestions. I was in the lobby when Stormy came in. Her tights were skin-tight and all she had carried was a phone with her credit card tucked in the back.

Melinda, well, just no. She had been kind to me. She had hugged me and said she didn't know what Todd had been thinking. That reminded me. What was it Todd had been mumbling in the jail cell about Melinda? My brain felt too addled to put it together.

"No, I don't remember her taking anything into the studio. Plus, she knew that you and Neil were there. That would have been pretty ballsy to plant poison in my closet with two sheriffs in the room."

"Ballsy?" Josie laughed. "You don't even sound like a yoga teacher."

I laughed with her. "Should I use that in class?"

"Yes!" CeCe jumped up, then mimicked me talking to my class. "'Students, try this ballsy pose as you lift your left leg and fling it behind you, tilting backwards as if you were having a panic attack. Which you will if you do this *ballsy* pose. And ... exhale.'"

I smiled at her. "One, I do not sound like that. Two, Wild Thing will not kill you and it's not all that ballsy. You're just afraid of it, so it has power over you."

CeCe rolled her eyes and then stretched both arms over her head. "So you say." She looked at her watch. "I need to get back to the shop to help close." She pulled me out of my chair and into her arms. "Love you, lady. Get some sleep tonight."

Josie and Cindy joined in their goodbyes. At the door, Cindy waved Josie through and paused, softly closing the door to turn to look at me.

"I'm so sorry, sis. I would give anything to take away everything you went through today. Sometimes my job …" her voice trailed off.

I smiled softly and walked into her arms, placing my head on her shoulder. "I know. Me, too. You're forgiven." I lifted my head and looked her in the eye. "But your hotshot detective is on the wrong trail, so I will do whatever I need to do to clear myself."

Cindy pursed her lips, then took a deep breath. "Fair enough."

She smiled sadly and slipped out the front door. I locked it behind her and leaned against it. I would clear myself, but now what?

Chapter 19

The seven o'clock class was small the next morning. Apparently, students had heard I'd been arrested, so they didn't show up. The ones who did come to class did not stay around to chat like they usually did. Not that I blamed them.

I quickly locked up behind the last student and slipped out the back, looking around to see if Stormy was going to make an appearance. She didn't, and I was oddly disappointed.

My car eased into the lot at Safety Blanket just as Jennifer was getting out of her car. She helped me unload the donations from the back of my SUV and carry them in.

"Thank you again, Mariah, for all your help. We really appreciate it." Jennifer set down the last bag of donations in a chair by her desk. When I didn't leave, her eyebrows raised. "Was there something else?"

"I just wanted to ask you about Patricia, if you have a minute."

She looked at her the watch on her fitness tracker and started to fuss with papers on her desk. "Just a minute, but I'm not sure what I can tell you. She only volunteered here a few times."

"What did she do here? IT stuff?"

She shook her head. "Not really. Of course, we have her sister, Melinda, to handle all of that. Melinda is a wiz at everything on the computer. She even developed a system to track our donations so we know exactly how much we bring in and where it goes. Mostly Patricia helped by logging donations in Melinda's system." Jennifer paused and smiled. "Melinda actually wasn't too happy about that."

"Why?"

"It seemed like there was some sibling rivalry going on." She shrugged and checked her watch again. "If you don't mind, I need to finish prepping for a meeting with our donors. It's not going to be pretty."

"Really? You guys do fundraisers all the time and I see all the good you are doing around town."

Jennifer nodded and leaned wearily against her desk. It was then that I noticed the dark rings under her eyes and stress lines around her lips. "You'd think, right? I don't know, but donations have fallen off and we're barely hanging on right now."

I left Jennifer in her office, surprised and saddened by the news. If Safety Blanket went out of business, needy moms and babies would have fewer resources. Maybe The Yoga Mat could hold another fundraiser. The thought hit me just as I got to my car, and I gave a rueful smile. The last fundraiser hadn't turned out too well. Maybe I'd better not be promising anything just yet. I hopped into the driver's seat and headed to CeCe's. It was coffee time.

I stretched my legs out long on the bench and rested my head on the back of the booth, one hand cupped around my coffee, the other playing with a pile of coffee stirrers someone had left on the table. CeCe would freak out about the waste if she found them.

Josie sat across from me, mirroring my position. "If this were San Francisco," she muttered, "we would know who threw a rock through your studio and we would have much more information about where everyone was."

"How so?" I didn't even open my eyes to ask.

"Security cameras. In big cities, you can't walk a half block down any street without showing up on someone's surveillance system."

"Who has been ruled out?"

Josie glanced toward the door as if worried Detective Samuelson was there. She leaned toward me, almost getting frosting on her uniform shirt. "Melinda and Allison have alibis, Stormy and Jennifer have no motive, so that leaves you and Todd McMillan."

I sat up but wouldn't look at her. My fingers absently played with the stirrers. "Seriously."

Josie shrugged. CeCe wandered over and sat down. I shoved the stirrers in my pocket.

"I remember Allison's alibi, since we uncovered it." CeCe flexed her bicep. "What's Melinda's alibi again?"

"She was at a conference in San Jose. Plus, she didn't show up on the security cameras outside Patricia's house. Of course, if it's between you and Todd, I think it's Todd."

I rolled my eyes, than cocked my head to look at Josie. "Is there a way to set it up so you don't show up on a security camera?"

Josie shrugged again. "If you know your way around the system, anything is possible."

A glimmer of excitement surged within me. Melinda had set up Patricia's security system as well as the one at Security Blanket. If anyone knew the ins and outs of the system, she did.

"How do you know for sure she was at the conference? It's not that far to drive. She could have driven there and back."

Josie sighed and shook her head. "Oddly enough, Mariah, we thought of that, being professionals at our jobs and all. She was in a bunch of photos on a social media site." She stood up and stretched. "See you ladies at the movie tonight."

We waved absently as Josie left, both of us deep in thought.

CeCe slipped out of the booth and went to her office, returning with a laptop. She started tapping at the keys, then looked up.

"She definitely was at the conference the night Patricia died. Look here."

I opened one eye to look. CeCe spun her laptop around on the table top. The screen was open to pictures on social media. She pointed from one to another. "See, here she is, and here she is, and here she is."

I sat up and stared into the screen, reaching for the scroll pad and flipping through the pictures on my own. "She sure is in a lot of pictures. If I were the suspicious type, I would say she wanted someone to see her. I mean, look, it's as if she just jumped into the middle of a bunch of people."

CeCe pointed to one photograph showing about five people all staring at Melinda. Indeed, the other women in the photograph looked surprised and a couple looked irritated to see Melinda take center stage as they posed.

CeCe scrolled through some more pictures. "I don't know a ton about the district attorney's office, but I would guess they wouldn't try to convict someone because they were photo hogs."

I barked out a laugh that caught in my throat. "Go back, go back." My voice took on an urgency. "No, keep going. Stop. Right there, right there."

"What? What are you seeing?" In the picture, Melinda had her hand on her left hip, her right arm thrown around a woman with a nametag and a badge. "I see nothing except how awkward they look. This conference must have tanked."

I reached over zoomed in to the pin on Melinda's chest. "Isn't that the pin Patricia bought for her? That she said she found on Patricia's desk?" I jumped out of the booth and began pacing back and forth in front of it. "Wasn't that the pin Patricia had stopped to show you the day she died?"

CeCe stared at the laptop, then slowly nodded. "That's the pin."

The pieces snapped into place in my mind. Melinda told us she was in San Jose all week, that she didn't get a chance to see her sister before she died.

"This picture was posted the night Patricia died. Melinda had to have seen her that day." I grabbed CeCe's hands. "She lied. She *lied.*"

We held tight to each other's hands, our eyes searching each other's. CeCe took a deep breath and disengaged from me, shaking out her hands. "Dang, you're strong."

I flexed my fingers. "Yoga."

She smiled.

"CeCe, are you sure you have the right day? People are in and out of here every day, sometimes" – I pointed to myself – "more than once."

She snapped her fingers. "She used a credit card. I can look up her credit card receipt."

"In your non-automated system?"

She looked toward her office and shrugged. "It might take a little time You can help." We stood in the doorway of her office and each took a deep breath.

"Tonight," I whispered to CeCe. "We will prove it tonight."

Chapter 20

Being small-business owners, we both were tied up the rest of the day. Between classes and private sessions, my calendar was full. CeCe was short-handed, since one of the baristas had gone home sick.

When I had a break mid-afternoon, I popped back over to the coffee shop for an afternoon pick-me-up, a chai tea latte made with almond milk. I sat on a stool by the bar sipping the sweet foam from the top.

"Mmmmm, this was exactly what I wanted."

CeCe just smiled and we both turned to look as the bell jingled above the door. Melinda Jacobs walked toward the counter.

"Mariah, I see you here more than I do at the yoga studio." She gave a belated smile.

"I'm going right now." I hopped down off the stool and started toward the door, pausing as I passed by.

"Oh, Melinda," I said, pausing as I looked at the front of her blazer. "That really is a lovely pin."

Melinda froze, her eyes flickering between my face and the pin. Then she gave a forced laugh. "Thank you. It reminds me of Patty."

I smiled and threw a wave to CeCe over my head.

By the time I had dropped off my basket for the silent auction, it was nearly seven o'clock when I finally managed to get back to CeCe's coffee shop, coming in the open back door because the front was closed for the night. CeCe handed me a pile of receipts and I started digging. "Have you thought about updating your system?" I muttered. "Maybe something electronic? We'll never get this done in time to get to the movie."

She shushed me with a wave. "I've had more important things to do. Besides it costs money to use electronic receipts. I haven't had a lot of extra cash sitting around to do that. And don't worry, we both know how this movie starts."

"Okay, but if they run out of the buttered popcorn before we get there, I will be irate or at least highly irritated. I've been looking forward to it all day."

CeCe shook her head. "Junk food will be the death of you."

"Junk food makes life worth living."

I sighed not quite silently and started flipping through the receipts. Finally, I landed on one for the same day Patricia died.

"Voila!" I exclaimed.

"You found it?"

"No, but I'm in the ballpark." I split the pile in half and shoved one half to her. Within a few moments, it was CeCe's turn to yell.

"Eureka!"

I looked up, cocking an eyebrow. "Eureka?"

"You already said 'Voila.' I couldn't very well say the same word. Then it would have no meaning."

She smirked, then peered closely at the small square sheet of paper, then looked up at me, her eyes sad. "It's the right day. Patricia came in the day she died and showed me the pin she had just bought."

She pulled out her phone and snapped a picture of the receipt. "What are you doing?" I asked.

"Taking a picture to send to Detective Hottie so he'll go arrest Melinda."

I narrowed my eyes. "I don't think it works like that."

She slumped down into her desk chair, tossing the phone on her desk. "I know, but I have to believe we just helped catch a killer."

Just then, a soft click startled us both. We turned to look at the door of CeCe's office to see Melinda Jacobs standing there holding a gun.

Chapter 21

"You wish you just helped catch a killer." Melinda smirked at us as she waved the gun. She walked over and snatched the receipt from CeCe's hand, then shoved it into her jeans pocket. She held out her hand for CeCe's phone. "I'll take that, too. That receipt means nothing since I'll get rid of it and I won't even need to explain it to him, what did you call him, 'Detective Hottie'?"

"Melinda, what are you doing with that gun?"

"What does it look like?" If a person can truly snarl, that's exactly what Melinda did. Her lips pulled back and her teeth bared. "I have to get rid of the evidence. Stand up, ladies, and come with me."

She waved her gun at us again, motioning for us to get up. We moved slowly. I don't know why CeCe was slow, but I figured it couldn't help but give me more time to think.

"Pick up the pace!" Melinda hissed at us. She reached for my arm and pulled me through the door, then pushed CeCe behind me, practically shoving us through the back door of the shop.

"Where are we going?" I asked as loud as I dared, hoping someone would be around to hear me.

She bumped my shoulder with the gun, propelling me forward. I'm sure I bruised.

"You'll die in this alley if you speak again, yoga lady. Shut up and walk."

We stayed in the alley for a few more blocks, not daring to speak. Melinda seemed a tad wound up. When CeCe started to shuffle to slow us down, Melinda banged CeCe's knee with the butt of the pistol. CeCe cried out in pain. Melinda hit her in the face.

Afraid to speak but worried about CeCe, I moved next to my friend and put my arms around her, turning to dare Melinda to stop me.

"Let's just go," CeCe whispered, her hand held to her cheek. I could see blood seep through her fingers.

"She's hurt." In response, Melinda lifted the gun and aimed it at my face. At the last moment, she pointed it near my feet and pulled the trigger. A soft pfffft sound and I felt something cut into my ankle, making me jump. I bit back a cry.

"Next time, I won't aim for your foot." Melinda motioned for us to continue walking.

With the silencer on her gun, Melinda had ensured that no one would hear the shots when she killed us, if that was what she planned – and I had to believe it was. Why else would she be forcing us to walk in the dark with a gun at our backs?

When we reached the end of the block, Melinda shoved the gun under her coat. She motioned for us to cross the street. I started to limp from where the bullet had grazed me and I held CeCe up as we crossed, the three of us moving slowly in a tight pack. Any other Saturday night, the street would have been busy but apparently everyone in town was at the movie in the recreation center at the other end of Main Street.

Melinda noticed it, too. "Perfect. I'll be able to dispose of you, then sneak back into my seat at the movie. I've seen it before, so if the cops ask, I'll be able to give them lots and lots of details. I even have popcorn waiting for me."

We trudged to the alley behind my building and to the back door of The Yoga Mat. "Open it," she ordered.

As I dug the key out of my pocket, I rubbed what felt like my bloody ankle on the side of the doorjamb. If we were to die here, I wanted to leave clues for Cindy and Josie. Once inside, Melinda wouldn't let me turn on the lights. CeCe leaned against the wall, then slid to the floor.

My phone buzzed and I tried not to glance at my pocket, where it was. "See who it is but don't swipe. I don't want you to have read it yet," Melinda ordered.

It was from Cindy. *When you are coming to the movie? It's starting.*

"What do you want me to say?"

"Nothing. Give me your phone."

She took my phone and stepping away from us, she typed. She smiled, then showed me the text. *Help. Todd McMillan is here with a gun.*

"Here's my plan." Melinda smiled. "You send the text. Then I shoot you both and slip out the back to the movies. By the time your sister the sheriff shows up, I'll be back in my seat eating popcorn."

CeCe whimpered.

Melinda shrugged. "I know. It's brilliant."

"Did you kill your sister so brilliantly, too?" If I was going to die, I wanted a few answers first. "How'd you do it?"

"You tell me, Miss Smarty Pants."

"You've been dousing her with arsenic that you were using to get rid of the gophers in your yard. You did it for a while now, am I right?"

Melinda nodded. "Every chance I got."

"You wanted her to suffer."

She shrugged and waved her gun as if to say "so what?"

"Her immune system got weaker and weaker."

She nodded again. "She was picking up all kinds of lovely bugs."

"You took the train to your conference, but drove back that day, after the panel you were on but before the mixer. You met Patricia at her house, accepted the pin she so thoughtfully picked out for you. Then you put the fatal dose of poison in her water bottle. You slipped onto the expressway and you were back in San Jose in a couple of hours."

Melinda clapped, using the pistol as the other hand. "Bravo, yoga lady. The truth really will set you free."

"But why?" I asked her. "And why here? I thought you enjoyed coming to The Yoga Mat."

"I did," she said earnestly. "I was actually quite sad that Patricia chose to die here. But I had to give her the fatal dose while I was at the conference. I couldn't be in town when she died. That makes sense, right? She was going to tell Todd any day now that she was going to divorce him." Sadness crept across her face. "He's a nice man. He doesn't deserve that. He deserves someone loyal, like me. I had planned to get him to marry me, but this will work, too."

"Your sister is dead and you're setting Todd up for murder."

She shrugged, which made me want to pound her face with the stray water bottle sitting on the floor. CeCe gently reached for my arm, shaking her head.

"She came to my house that first week, babbling about how peaceful and serene it was here and how she thought she could finally find her own path through yoga." She sneered. "At first, I just laughed at her. I've been doing yoga for years. I know all about downward dog poses. I went to her house one day to find her with her legs up on the walls. She said it was calming and rejuvenating. She said I should try it some time, that it would do me good." She rolled her eyes. "I already knew all that."

"Yoga is more than just the physical poses, Melinda."

Melinda scoffed as she paced back and forth in front of us. "She had everything – and she wanted to toss it away. Are you kidding me? I wondered, when was it my turn?" She turned toward me and leaned in violently. "So I decided to take my turn."

I sank back into the bolsters to get away from her, then realization struck and I sat up. "You started stealing from Safety Blankets. That's where all this extra money came from – and Patricia found out. That's the real reason you killed her. It wasn't about the yoga at all."

Melinda backed away, shaking the gun up and down as she began to pace in front of us. She stopped and held the gun to her cheek lovingly.

"That organization makes thousands and thousands of extra dollars. They weren't going to miss a few thousand here and there."

"You siphoned it off the top."

She winked at me. *Yes, winked.* I nearly threw up.

"Even better. I set up a program to divert funds to an off-shore account. Jennifer and her chirpy little minions didn't even know they were supposed to receive the money. Poor Jennifer kept looking for new ways to fund-raise and, ha ha ha, nothing seemed to be paying off the way she thought it would."

CeCe struggled to sit up. "Stay there!" Melinda barked. CeCe slumped back down, her eyes wide in terror.

"How did Patricia figure it out?" I tried to draw Melinda's attention back to me.

The gun whipped back toward me. I flinched. Melinda smiled. She studied me as if weighing what to say.

"She volunteered at the office. Jennifer mentioned the money problem, so Patricia started poking her nose into my business, said she was seeing if she could make things more efficient. She started asking me questions about my programs."

"And," I continued. "You reset the security system at Patricia's house so it wouldn't show that you had been there at all."

Melinda gave a slight bow. "It does pay to be an IT expert."

"But your sister is still dead."

"She had it coming. It wasn't just that she threatened to turn me in." She paced back and forth, then turned and looked at me. "She killed our parents, you know. Called them up crying about how she was divorcing her husband. Again. They jumped into the car and hit the freeway, racing up here to take care of their baby. They died because of her."

I caught my breath at the viciousness and sadness of the energy that flowed from Melinda. "Don't you think she felt bad about that, too?"

"No!" She screamed. "She was about to go and do it again. Husband Number Five?" She gave an "out" sign like a major league umpire. "He's outa there! She'll get his money and the house and move on to the next one." She stopped and smirked, tapping the gun against her hand. "Except she won't, will she?"

Her eyes welled up with tears, catching both of us off-guard. "There won't be a Husband Number Six for Patricia." She sniffed as tears fell down her cheeks, wiping them off with the sleeve of her blouse.

Taking a deep and ragged breath, she wiped my phone off with the edge of her sweater, then without touching it again handed it back to me. "Press *send*. If you try anything else, I will torture your friend before you die."

The coldness of this woman swept through me. As I took the phone, I quickly and quietly began doing a *ujjayi* breath to heat my insides and fight the cold that embraced Melinda Jacobs.

She aimed the gun at me. As I reached for the phone and pressed the *send* button, I grabbed a bolster from behind me, flinging it at Melinda with all my might. From the corner of my eye, I saw her jaw tighten and she pulled the trigger. My body flew backward into the wall and my eyes closed. More gunshots sounded, and I was sure Melinda had killed CeCe. I could no longer hold on. I fell into blackness.

Chapter 22

"Sis, sis, Mariah, can you hear me?"

I opened my eyes to see Cindy's face practically touching my nose. Her arms were around me and she was cradling me in her lap. Tears poured down her face, which looked streaked with blood. Stormy knelt next to her, her face moving back and forth as she tried to see mine.

"I'm not dead?"

Cindy shook her head, smiling weakly through her tears.

"She shot me. I know I hit the wall. I can still feel it." I struggled to sit up. Cindy helped me.

I was surprised to see a flurry of activity in my studio. Sheriff's deputies and paramedics hurried back and forth across the room. Somewhere in the back of my mind, I noted they had not taken off their shoes, but at the moment I didn't care.

"CeCe?" I tried to turn to look where she had been, grimacing from pain in my side and back. CeCe lay propped against the wall, an emergency medical technician on either side. Her eyes fluttered.

"She's going to be okay. The paramedics are with her." Cindy kept one arm around my back to hold me up and pointed with her other arm.

"What happened? How come I'm not dead? She shot me." The realization that I nearly died hit me and I began to tremble uncontrollably.

"Can I get a blanket over here?" Cindy called to a deputy, who disappeared for a moment, then reappeared with a woolen blanket. They wrapped it around me and let me lean back into the bolsters. Cindy held one up. It had a gash in one side.

"Apparently, you deflected a bullet with this bolster, but another one hit your side and the force knocked you on your butt into the wall." She smiled affectionately.

Two paramedics stepped toward me, Neil Samuelson following in their wake. They kneeled at my side, gently lifting my shirt to look at the wound on my hip. Neil pulled a bolster from the pile and sat down.

I turned to him with more questions. "How did you know where we were?" I grimaced as the paramedic poured liquid into my gunshot wound. Now there's a sentence I never expected in my repertoire.

Neil held up a small plastic bag that appeared to hold several coffee stir sticks for CeCe to see. "Any idea where these came from?"

CeCe frowned weakly. "Are those from my shop?"

Samuelson dramatically swung the bag in my direction. "Then it must have been you." It wasn't a question.

My brain still felt foggy as I stared at the bag. I had no idea what he was talking a-

"Oh, right." I started to giggle. I caught myself and cleared my throat, looking straight at the EMT next to me. "I don't giggle. Did you give me something?"

She looked at me with raised eyebrows and continued her work.

I hesitated, then looked back at CeCe. "Today, when you were getting your laptop, some slob-"

"You mean customer?" CeCe interjected.

I frowned at her "Yes, some *customer* tried to build a castle with a pile of stirrers on their table."

Neil, CeCe and the EMT stopped to look at me

"Okay, it was me. I got a little bored. *Anyway*, when you came back into the shop," I nodded toward CeCe, "I picked them up and shoved them into my pocket so you wouldn't find out. I forgot about them until we were being force-marched down the alley, I started dropping coffee sticks. It was the only thing I could think of to do that wouldn't get you hurt."

CeCe and I smiled widely, if weakly, at each other.

"For a yoga teacher, you're kind of a slob."

"That's fair." I giggled again and looked at the EMT with wide eyes.

She shook her head. "It's probably just stress. It will pass." Her voice sounded serious, but her lips looked like they were fighting off a smile.

Neil picked up the rest of the story. "I wasn't sure it was a trail, but I didn't have anything else to go on after CeCe sent me the receipt picture. It was clearly taken in your office, CeCe, but when I got there, no one was there. You left all the lights on and the back door was unlocked, and..." He paused apparently for dramatic effect. "Papers were piled in a big mess all over your office. That's when I knew for sure something was wrong."

CeCe leaned back against the wall and grimaced, then smiled. "It pays to be a little OCD."

"Then Stormy came running around the corner of the building, saying Melinda Jacobs had you in the studio." Neil gestured toward Stormy, who gave a little wave.

"Wait a minute. You were still spying on me? Why?"

Stormy shrugged sheepishly. "The deputies seemed to imply that you set me up at the Old Gym, and I couldn't be sure you weren't

Patricia's killer. I figured I'd better keep an eye on you. When you weren't at the movie, I came looking for you."

We smiled at each other. "Thank goodness you did." My voice broke and I held out my arms to Stormy, who gently eased into them. I patted her head. "You saved us, Stormy. Thank you."

Stormy struggled back to her knees, smiling through the tears as she wiped them from her face.

"CeCe!" We all turned toward the voice at the doorway to see Paul the barista, who screeched to a halt at the door of the studio when he saw me. He looked down at his shoes. I waved him in. I was going to have to clean the floor anyway.

Paul rushed to CeCe's side and took her hand. They smiled into each other's eyes. So much for not being a "big deal" relationship.

I turned back to Neil and Cindy. "What happened next?"

They took turns retelling the story. When Cindy received the text about Todd McMillan, she freaked out and called Neil. "Then Neil mentioned he had a patrol car sitting outside McMillan's house and that McMillan hadn't left, so it couldn't have been him."

Cindy and Neil had snuck around to the back door of The Yoga Mat and Cindy used her key to unlock the back to slip inside. Then Neil and Josie took the key and went around to the front.

"We heard Melinda's confession. That's when we bolted through the doors and saw Melinda fire at you."

Cindy reached over and caressed my cheek and forehead. "We had to take her out."

My mouth fell open, although I think some part of me already knew. I nodded silently and let my head fall onto Cindy's shoulder. "She killed Patricia and tried to kill you, sis. After she shot at you, she turned the gun on us. We had to."

The EMT touched my hand and helped me stand up to get on the gurney that had rolled across my studio floor. My floor!

I twisted out of her grasp to survey the damage and was dismayed to see black streaks from the lobby door to where we stood. My shoulders slumped.

Cindy pushed me onto the gurney. "Now is not the time to worry about the floor." I wanted to argue but felt overcome by weariness.

I nodded and sank back on to the padding. I remember weakly waving to CeCe, who was being helped onto a gurney of her own before I felt myself sink into a welcoming blackness.

Chapter 23

I walked gingerly to the front door of The Yoga Mat, placing my hand against the glass window. Taking a deep breath, I turned the key, then swung open the front door.

Silence but not coldness greeted me. The lamp was on in the studio. Warmth emanated into the lobby and I could smell a citrusy odor from the defuser on the table in the corner. I slipped off my boots and stepped inside the studio.

A gentle smile spread across my face and tears pricked at my eyes. I hadn't known what to expect and this sense of coming home caught me by surprise. Every doubt that I'd ever had about moving to Jasper and opening my studio disappeared. Whether or not I succeeded, I had found my place in the world, at least for now.

The soft shush of the door behind me called my attention and I turned back to the lobby. Cindy's face peeked out of the office as Josie, Stormy, Neil and Jason quietly stepped inside, smiles filling their faces.

"How did we do?" Cindy couldn't wait to ask.

I walked back to the lobby and opened my arms, bringing them all in for one big hug. "It's beautiful. Thank you."

"Did you even notice the floor?" Neil pointed into the studio. "It took hours to clean that up."

Cindy had held a modified list of classes while I had been recuperating from my wounds. Tabitha had resigned, saying the studio was not "yoga enough" for her, what with people being killed and bricks being thrown through the windows. I was nearly ready to come back part time.

The five kicked off their shoes and stuck them in the cubbies, then headed inside the studio. Jason started to unroll his mat.

"Um. What are you doing?" I watched as the others set up, too.

Neil looked at the clock. "It's almost noon. Time for class."

I looked at each of them in turn. "I wasn't expecting to teach a class yet."

Cindy laughed as she set her mat down at the front. "I was. Now grab a mat. Do only what feels right."

The front door softly opened. Todd McMillan hesitantly stepped through. He paused when he saw me, then took a deep breath and shuffled toward me.

My shoulders tightened up and I started to step away from him, stepping on Neil's foot. He had slipped up behind me when Todd walked in.

Todd held a yoga mat in front of himself like a shield and spoke quietly. "I owe you an apology. I'm sorry that I thought you had killed Patricia and I tried to ruin your business. I left a check that should cover the cost of repairing your window." He held up the mat in his hands. "Patricia really loved this place. The sheriff thought it would be okay if I stayed for class."

I nodded, then reached out and took Todd's hand. "Thank you. Welcome to The Yoga Mat." Just then Stormy stepped in and helped Todd find a cubby for his shoes and set up his mat in the studio.

Neil put his hand on my shoulder as I finally exhaled. I felt him lean in close to me. He spoke softly. "Melinda was the one who kept feeding him bad information, telling him that you had done it. She got him to throw the brick through your window."

I patted his hand, grateful for his help.

Just then the door opened and two of my regular yoga students stepped in. They quickly took off their shoes and slipped across the floor to me, lightly embracing me as if aware of my injuries.

Before I could talk with them, the door opened again and another student came in, then another and another. Within ten minutes, the class was nearly full, students talking excitedly to each other. Stormy hovered by Cindy near the office door, helping with student payments as Cindy talked with other students.

I raised my eyebrows. "Stormy has been helping out with classes since Tabitha quit," Cindy said. "She's been handling the money and the website so I could focus on teaching. She's been a huge help these past few weeks while you've been recuperating." She put an arm around Stormy and pulled her in.

My eyes filled with tears and I reached over to join in. Stormy shrugged awkwardly out of our hug and looked around the studio.

"It was the least I could do. Maybe I can help some more when you come back full time?" Her eyes looked hopeful.

I smiled and nodded. "Absolutely. Welcome to the team. We'll figure out the details later."

As the noon hour approached, Cindy dimmed the lights to begin. I sat down lightly on my mat just inside the door of the studio. I was home. My shoulders relaxed as I inhaled, then exhaled.

Namaste.

About the author

When Jacqueline M. Green first heard of "cozy mysteries," she thought her sister had brilliantly made up the term. She was delighted to discover it was a genre all its own, with tons of stories about crafting, quilting, knitting and cooking, but alas, few about yoga. As a writer, yoga instructor and lover of mysteries, she decided to solve that problem or at least add to the yoga cozies in the world. She lives with her family plus two cats, a dog and a fish (that may or may not still be alive).

Made in the USA
Coppell, TX
24 June 2020